Diana took a deep breath and looked directly into Torrie's eyes.

"It's not that simple, Torrie. I feel more for you than friendship, and the very idea scares me to death! I've no right to have such feelings. I'm a nun. I'm certainly not a . . . a . . . lesbian. No matter how I feel about you, I'm not a lesbian." Diana felt the heat in her face and knew she was blushing.

"How do you feel about me, Diana?" Torrie brushed the tears from Diana's cheeks.

"I don't even know how to express it." Diana felt embarrassed and relieved at the same time. "I want to touch you . . . to feel your body against mine."

D1051288

Forever

by Evelyn Kennedy

Forever

by Evelyn Kennedy

THE NAIAD PRESS, INC.
1995

Printed in the United States of America on acid-free paper
First Edition

Edited by Christine Cassidy
Cover design by Bonnie Liss (Phoenix Graphics)
Typeset by Sandi Stancil

Library of Congress Cataloging-in-Publication Data

Kennedy, Evelyn, 1939–
   Forever / by Evelyn Kennedy.
      p.   cm.
   ISBN 1-56280-094-9
   I. Title.
PS3561.E4263F67   1995
813'.54—dc20   94-41110
                                             CIP

*To each of us who finds the wisdom
to listen to her heart;
and gathers the courage to follow it.*

About the Author

Evelyn Kennedy brings a varied background to the art of fiction. She holds a Ph.D. in psychology, an M.Div. in theology and an M.Ed. in educational psychology. She spent several years as a cloistered nun, completed a tour of duty as a paramedic with the U.S. Armed Forces, taught in universities and schools of nursing, and holds a brown belt in karate. She is a military historian who is committed to revealing the truth about women's military history. She writes poetry and collects old movies. Her first three novels, *Cherished Love, Of Love and Glory,* and *To Love Again,* all published by Naiad Press, were best-sellers. The two main characters from *Cherished Love* play a role in her latest novel, *Forever.*

Books by Evelyn Kennedy

Cherished Love
Of Love and Glory
To Love Again
Forever

CHAPTER 1

Sister Diana Colletti looked at her watch. She had exactly 22 minutes to get lunch before her scheduled meeting with her new preceptor and the rest of the nurse practitioner's intern group at Emory University Hospital.

She made her selections quickly, a chef's salad with blue cheese dressing on the side, and hurried to the beverage section of the hospital cafeteria. She pushed a large glass against the trigger of an ice machine and wished the ice cubes would fall faster. She filled the glass with ice water, lifted her tray and

1

turned to her left without looking up. There was a loud sound of silverware hitting the tile floor as Diana ran, tray first, into a tall, dark-haired woman wearing a lab coat and carrying a tray. Diana watched in embarrassment as the woman's salad, and what appeared to be butterscotch pudding, collided with the starched lab coat and ran down in colorful, lumpy butterscotch streams.

"I'm so sorry," Diana said. She placed her tray on the cafeteria rail, grabbed a handful of paper napkins and turned again toward the woman. "Let me help you clean up this mess. I'll be happy to buy you another lunch."

Diana felt self-conscious. The woman's green eyes were staring at her, bright with anger and annoyance.

Diana used several napkins to remove two butterscotch-coated carrot slices and several pieces of iceberg lettuce from the starched cotton of the woman's white coat.

"If you want to clean up, I'll get you another tray," Diana said.

"That's not necessary," the woman said. She put her tray on the rail next to Diana's and took the paper napkins from Diana's hand. "I really don't have time for lunch anyway." The woman dabbed at the mess.

"I'm really sorry," Diana said. "I'm afraid I was in such a hurry, I just didn't look before I turned around."

Diana was relieved to see that the anger had left the woman's eyes. "At least let me pay for your lunch tomorrow."

"Thank you," the woman said. A smile slid across

her face, disappearing as quickly as it had appeared. "Don't worry about it. Accidents happen." She threw her last handful of napkins into a trash basket and looked down at her lab coat. "I think I'd better change if I don't want to be mistaken for a sloppy chef."

Diana looked at her watch. "I have to run too." She smiled at the woman. "If we meet again, I owe you the lunch of your choice."

"I'll keep that in mind," she said, turning and walking quickly toward the door.

Diana looked at her watch. There wasn't enough time left to eat lunch. She took a deep breath and headed for the meeting.

In room 418 Diana joined seven other registered nurses waiting anxiously to meet their preceptors and begin their internship as nurse practitioners. She smiled and nodded to several of them, introduced herself to two others and made her way to a seat at the front of the room. There was a large blackboard, a movie screen, a lectern, several anatomy charts and above the blackboard, a large electric wall clock. She watched as the minute hand jumped forward and landed on the black mark indicating the exact hour.

They're late, she thought. She needn't have hurried so. Her mind drifted. What was it Reverend Mother had told her about attending Emory? "No need to be in a hurry, Sister." She would be more use, Reverend Mother had continued, to the hospital in Kenya as a nurse practitioner than a general duty R.N. "Patience is one of the virtues you still have to learn." After all, Diana thought, the order knew what it was doing by requiring her to complete the internship at Emory before she returned to Africa.

She looked at the wall clock again. Three minutes after the hour. Her stomach growled and she wished she hadn't skipped breakfast . . . and lunch. With luck the meeting wouldn't last long and she could stop by the cafeteria and get a frozen yogurt or a salad.

There was the sound of people getting to their feet, and people walking toward the front of the room.

Diana watched as the small group filed onto the raised platform in front of the room. Of the eight physicians on the stage, two were women, and one of them was the woman Diana had run into in the cafeteria.

I don't believe this, Diana thought. Of all the people to crash into, she had to pick a staff member of the nurse practitioner intern team.

"Good afternoon," one of the men began. "My name is Dr. James Baldwin. I'm the chief of this program, and it's my pleasure to welcome you to Emory University, and the nurse practitioner internship program. Each of you has earned a place here by surpassing more than one hundred competitors. Competitors who were at the top in their particular areas. You were chosen over them because you are the best of the best."

He paused for a moment, beaming at them, then continued, "Each physician who acts as a preceptor in this program does so because he or she is committed to seeing you reach your full potential. Each is a preceptor because teaching has a special significance

4

to him or her. They believe, as I do, that physicians have a unique obligation to see to it that the best-trained medical personnel are provided to the people of our nation and to the world. In the full recognition of that obligation, I and my colleagues pledge to you that when you graduate from this program, you will be the very best nurse practitioners that this fine university knows how to produce." Dr. Baldwin's warm smile added a relaxed atmosphere to the room.

"To help bring about that objective, each of you has been assigned an individual mentor — an individual preceptor — to help you reach the goal you have set for yourself, and the high standards set for you by this university. As part of your welcome, there will be a buffet dinner tonight at 6:30 PM at Dr. Victoria Lassiter's home. Directions are on the back table. You can pick up a copy on your way out."

He slipped on a pair of half-glasses and looked out at the group from over the wireless rim. "Now, let me introduce your individual preceptors to you. As I call your names, please come to the right of the stage and meet your preceptor. You are then free until 6:30 this evening when we will see you for dinner." He took several sheets of paper from his inside pocket and began to read. "Dr. Ronald Abbott is the preceptor for Jean Northcutt."

Diana watched as Doctor Abbott and Jean Northcutt moved toward the right side of the stage.

Diana's stomach rumbled again — four hours until dinner — as the official pairing off progressed. Then she saw the woman from the cafeteria rise.

"Dr. Victoria Lassiter," Dr. Baldwin read. Diana snapped to attention as he finished his sentence. ". . . the preceptor for Sister Diana Colletti."

This must be like winning the lottery in reverse, Diana thought as she walked toward Dr. Lassiter and shook her hand.

"Welcome, Sister," she said. "I believe we've met before."

Diana felt the heat rising from her neck to her face. "I'm glad to see I'll have an opportunity to make up for this afternoon."

Dr. Lassiter laughed. "There's nothing to make up for. But if it bothers you, you can buy lunch before your internship is over. But for tonight, you're the guest."

"It sounds like fun. I'm looking forward to it."

"Good," Dr. Lassiter said. "Now if you'll excuse me, I have another meeting in five minutes. I'll see you this evening." Without another word, she walked to the door and disappeared from the room.

Diana stood for a moment looking in Dr. Lassiter's direction. She's certainly direct and to the point, she thought. Oh, well, it gave her time to get some frozen yogurt and straighten the apartment up a bit.

CHAPTER 2

Diana found Dr. Lassiter's house with no trouble. The woman gives great directions, Diana thought as she parked her white Chevette behind the silver Mercedes in the driveway. She switched off the ignition and looked at the house. English Tudor was one of Diana's favorite styles of architecture. Ivy covered the entire facade — except for the brick-red front door and the large windows that reminded her of islands set in a dark green sea. Brick-red was a perfect contrast for the light and dark green leaves of the old oak and poplars that stood like an army of sentries in the large front lot.

Diana walked slowly up the cobblestone driveway past several other cars, admiring the four-foot-high Bufurdi hollies that ran like a fence across the front of the house. The unmanicured, natural state of the property was exactly what Diana would have chosen if the house were her own.

She rang the bell and was welcomed in immediately by Dr. James Baldwin. He was wearing a chef's apron over his button-down collared white shirt.

"Diana Colletti, isn't it?" he said. He handed her a stick-on name tag and ushered her in the direction of laughter and voices engaged in several different conversations. He stopped just inside a large family room. "Help yourself to the buffet."

"Thank you," Diana said. "Can I help with anything?"

"Tonight you're a guest." Dr. Baldwin smiled at her lively brown eyes. "Just mingle and have a good time."

Diana took a plate, filled it sparingly, and joined her colleagues.

"This is so nice," Jean Northcutt said. "Very thoughtful of Emory to bring us together like this."

"Emory didn't bring you together." The voice came from behind Diana. "The buffet was Dr. Baldwin's idea."

Diana turned and saw Victoria Lassiter walking toward the group. Her tan slacks and forest green tailored blouse outlined her trim figure perfectly.

"Enjoy it," Dr. Lassiter said. "Once your program begins tomorrow, you'll have little time for social events."

"Honestly, Torrie, are you trying to frighten them to death? The program is tough, but it's not basic training for Navy SEALS." The statement came from a woman Diana hadn't seen before. She was about an inch taller than Dr. Lassiter and had an engaging smile.

"Ladies," Dr. Lassiter said. "This is Dr. Joan Kelly. She's one of Atlanta's leading allergists — and an unabashed optimist."

The group laughed and Diana made a note of Victoria Lassiter's ability to charm people — even those who barely knew her. The conversations in the room resumed, and Diana found herself on the periphery of a group of four who were discussing the problems of finding good child care. Her mind wandered and she found herself overhearing the conversation between Dr. Lassiter and Dr. Kelly who stood immediately behind her.

"Optimistic enough to take Mark Mason's referral of you for an allergy work-up. And realistic enough to think the man deserves an award for being your personal primary physician. He assured me that you will keep your appointment in Baltimore in five weeks," Joan Kelly said. She looked at her watch. "And optimistic enough to believe I can still make it downtown in time for the first act of *La Boheme.*" Joan Kelly checked her watch and then kissed Dr. Lassiter on the cheek. "I'll see you Saturday at one. Don't stand me up."

"I wouldn't dare," Dr. Lassiter said.

Diana's group drifted off toward the dessert table, leaving Diana standing alone. She sat down in a nearby chair and continued eating. The discussion between the two physicians continued.

"I don't see why this can't wait until the school term is finished."

Joan Kelly's expression changed to one of exasperation. She put her hand on Victoria's arm and stopped her in mid-stride.

"Don't start again, Torrie." Joan Kelly's voice sounded stern. "We've been over this a hundred times. We've gone as far as we can go in Atlanta in determining which allergens are causing your migraines. If you really want to find the triggers and eliminate them, you're going to have to go to an allergist and a clinic more specialized than me and Emory. Russ Kirkland and his group at Johns Hopkins are as good as it gets. I had to pull a lot of strings to get you a work-up in just five weeks. They have the top people in every specialty right there, so if you need any consults, you can get them during the same visit." Dr. Kelly looked directly into Torrie's eyes. "It really did take all the influence Mark Mason and I could muster to get you in so fast. Their next regular work-up appointment isn't for three months, and judging from your headaches, that three months could seem like a year. So just accept the fact that Kirkland and the clinic aren't going to come to you. You will have to go to Baltimore."

Dr. Lassiter held her hands up as if surrendering. "I'm going — I'm going," she said. "For four days only. If they can't figure it out in that time, I'll just have to live with it."

"They'll find the triggers, I guarantee it." She chuckled. "But after having you as a patient for four days, they'll probably never take another referral from me."

"I'll be on my best behavior, I promise."

10

"I'll believe that when it happens," Joan Kelly said. "You're not exactly anyone's dream patient." She turned and walked out of the room.

Joan Kelly's departure left Diana alone with Dr. Lassiter. Diana arose, ready to discard her empty plate.

"Well, Sister, it looks as if you'll have to be adopted out for about five days of your program," Dr. Lassiter's face was serious. Clearly she knew that Diana had overheard the entire conversation. "I hate that. I pride myself on being available to my students." Dr. Lassiter's eyes glanced away. "Maybe I can get the date changed by calling Baltimore myself. Even if I do have to wait a few months." She looked directly at Diana. "Maybe you won't have to be adopted out after all."

Diana felt amusement and concern with Dr. Lassiter's comments. "Please don't do that on my account. I'm a very good student. I can't imagine that five days without your actual presence would sink my program." Diana hoped that what she was about to say wouldn't offend her preceptor, but one way or the other, she had already decided she had to say it. "I realize you haven't asked my opinion, but I agree with Dr. Kelly. You need to keep your appointment and find out which allergens are causing the headaches. I don't believe any time will actually suit you, whether it's five weeks or five months from now." She smiled. "You just don't like the idea of being away from your work."

Dr. Lassiter's expression was a mixture of surprise and disbelief. She stared at Diana, her mouth open.

Now I've really done it, Diana thought. In her experience no physician was secure enough to take

11

the truth from a "mere" nurse, let alone her student. Well, it was too late now. She'd crossed her Rubicon.

"Look, I'm sorry if I offended you," Diana said. "I couldn't help overhearing the conversation. Please don't use me as an excuse to change your appointment. You'll find very quickly that I'm an excellent student and won't suffer irreparable damage from your five days' absence."

"Are you always so blunt, Sister?"

"Pretty much," Diana said. "I find it easier than pretending." She shrugged. "I guess it's not smart politics, but I'm not sure I can play politics. In fact, I don't even want to try."

"What about your career? How do you expect to get ahead without playing politics to some extent?" Dr. Lassiter asked.

"Getting ahead isn't a goal for me," Diana said. "I would never have become a nun if I were concerned with getting ahead."

"Sometime you'll have to tell me just why you did become a nun. I'm afraid I know almost nothing about such things." She smiled. "You haven't offended me. Surprised me, but not offended me. I respect your honesty, but not everyone at Emory will. If you want to get out of here as a nurse practitioner, be careful whom you shower with truth."

Diana felt that Dr. Lassiter was being not only straightforward, but kind. "Thank you," Diana said. "I'll keep that in mind."

"Good. And I do feel you're right about keeping that appointment." She grinned. "I also believe you're right about my absence not doing you any damage. I wish all my students were like that." She glanced around the room. "I think I'd better visit with the

12

rest of my guests," she said. "I certainly look forward to working with you, Sister. I'll see you in my office tomorrow at eight o'clock."

"Thank you," Diana said. "I'll be there at eight sharp." She met Dr. Lassiter's eyes. "Could I ask you a favor?"

"Certainly." Dr. Lassiter nodded.

"Please call me Diana. 'Sister' sounds awfully formal."

"Fine. And please call me Torrie. My parents are the only ones who call me Victoria, and then it's when they're angry at me or want to make a particular point." She extended her hand. "I look forward to working with you. Bright, committed students always make my job a lot easier, and a lot more of a challenge."

CHAPTER 3

Over the next five weeks, Torrie and Diana saw each other at the hospital every day. Torrie was proud of Diana Colletti. She learned quickly, had a good bedside manner with patients, and an exceptionally gentle touch when examining patients in pain or when performing necessary, painful procedures.

What teacher wouldn't be proud of a student's professional abilities, Torrie thought as she observed Diana examine an eleven-year-old boy who had been referred to Emory's Egleston Hospital. No diagnosis was given to any nurse practitioner, only the patient's name, age and presenting complaint. It was the job of the nurse practitioner to examine the patient, make an assessment, determine a diagnosis and a plan for treatment and care.

Diana was listening to the boy's chest.

"I'm hearing a continuous murmur," she said as she moved the stethoscope. "The murmur is loudest at the left upper sternal border and clavicle." Diana looked up from the boy. "That along with the bounding posterior tibial and dorsalis pedis pulses lead me to the diagnosis of patent ductus arteriosus."

"Well done," Torrie said. "You picked up the heart sounds exactly right." She was particularly impressed with Diana's ability to make diagnoses.

Unless I'm missing an awful lot, Torrie thought, she's just about perfect. She wondered if all nuns were like her, or if she was an exception, even to their rules.

"We have about thirty minutes to review your work this week," Torrie said as they walked across the sky bridge from Egleston to Emory's main hospital. "When I get back from Baltimore, we'll review your week. I've set aside an hour on the Tuesday after I return."

"That sounds fine," Diana said. "I'll keep notes on any questions that come up."

They reached Torrie's office and Diana relaxed in the large upholstered chair in front of the desk.

"Would you like a cup of coffee?" Torrie asked.

"Yes. I'll get it," Diana said. She jumped to her feet. "Why don't you sit down? You look tired."

"Thanks," Torrie said. The headache must show, she thought. She opened the top right-hand drawer of her desk and took one Tylenol with Codeine from a plastic prescription bottle. She threw it into her mouth and washed it down with a long swallow of ice water that could always be found in an oversized thermal cup she kept nearby. She closed her eyes and pressed her fingertips against her temples.

"Your headache must be pretty bad," Diana said. "Can I get you something for it?" She placed the mug of coffee on Torrie's desk.

Torrie opened her eyes and looked at her. Diana's short brown hair fell in natural ringlets against the smooth olive skin of her forehead. Even without make-up, her long dark lashes drew attention to the alert intelligence of her velvet brown eyes. She looked at least 5 years younger than the 30 years indicated on her application to the program. "Thanks, I just took something. I'll be fine in a minute." She leaned forward. "Let's talk about work."

Diana sat down again in the overstuffed chair. "I feel that everything is going great. What I'm learning about cardiovascular diagnosis will be absolutely invaluable to me when I get back to Kenya. I'll be able to refer cardiac patients to Johannesburg and the U.S. when it's necessary. The Church and private donors will pay for travel, hospitalization and surgery."

Diana's face lit up as she spoke. Torrie recognized the passion, passion for life and passion for work. These were clearly Diana's mission.

"I think you're a very talented diagnostician," Torrie said. "I've seen a lot of nurse practitioners, a lot of interns and residents pass through Emory. None of them has had your gift for diagnosis."

"That's a real compliment. Thank you," Diana

said. "It does a lot to boost my confidence for my work in Kenya."

"You've earned it. I think you'll do very well in Kenya. They'll be lucky to have you." Torrie took a small swallow of coffee. "In fact, I wish I had more students like you."

"I'll put in a good word for you with Reverend Mother. Who knows, you may become the first and last word in training nuns in the area."

"That's enough to make me reconsider my statement," Torrie said. "But I have a feeling you're not the average nun."

"Maybe not," Diana said. "But then, you're not the average preceptor. I've listened and watched you very closely over the past weeks. You're so caring and patient in explaining concepts and procedures, explaining them in different ways until I understood them." Diana took a sip from her coffee cup. "Some professors just repeat the same idea over and over. But you seem completely comfortable with whatever it takes to get what you're teaching across to your student. I feel fortunate to have you as my mentor."

"We sound like a mutual admiration society," Torrie said. "But I'm afraid I have to draw our session to a close. I'll be leaving in four days and I still don't have someone to housesit with Winston." She glanced at the photo of the silver and black Yorkshire terrier on her desk. He was standing on the beige carpet in the family room, trying to pull an orange rubber bone toward him.

"You don't put him in a kennel when you go out of town?" Diana asked.

"No. I prefer to have someone come to the house and spend some time with Winston. It's much less

17

upsetting to Winston. But my usual dog-sitter is out of town."

"I'd be glad to take care of him for you while you're gone. He already knows me from the time our class met at your house. I know we'd get along fine."

"Are you serious?" Torrie asked.

"Sure. I like him. We can keep each other company, and it will get me out of my one-room apartment for a little while each day and take my mind off the problems with my lease."

"Great!" Torrie was relieved. "Why don't you stay in the guest room while I'm gone? That would be even better for Winston, and you'd have the run of the house."

"Fine with me if it's okay with you."

"I'd feel a whole lot better about going to Baltimore." She had an idea. "In fact, why don't you come by after work tomorrow. I'll pick up a couple of deli sandwiches for us, and I'll show you where Winston's food and vitamins are kept."

They arranged a time, and Diana gathered her things. "By the way," Diana said, "I like mustard on my sandwiches."

CHAPTER 4

Torrie paid for her coffee and scanned the cafeteria.

"Over here, Torrie." The voice came from her left. She turned to see Doctor Megan McKenzie waving at her.

Torrie waved back and made her way to Megan's table.

"That was a fantastic job you did this morning," Torrie said. "I wouldn't have given that patient more than a ten percent chance for survival." Torrie looked at Megan McKenzie and felt respect and admiration. "You're one hell of a surgeon."

Megan smiled and nodded. "Thank you, Doctor. You could be every bit as good if you'd give up some of your teaching duties and concentrate on cardiovascular surgery."

"I like teaching too much to give it up," Torrie said.

"Not even a fourth of it?" Megan asked.

"Not even a fourth."

"You and Lynn are two of a kind," Megan said. "Lynn wouldn't give up her teaching appointment even for a practice with twice the money and half the patients."

"Would you really want her to stop teaching?"

"Not really," Megan said. "It's part of her charm. Both of you are very good in the classroom. Sometimes I wonder if the students know how lucky they are."

"That's not important," Torrie said. "It only matters that they become good physicians, or good nurse practitioners. That's what makes it worthwhile."

"Lynn talked to Mark Mason a couple of days ago," Megan said. "He said the clinic is really taking shape."

Torrie nodded. "It's looking very good. We'll start seeing patients in Saint Cloud in about six weeks."

"Just you and Mark?" Megan asked. "Surely you'll need additional help. At least one good nurse, or nurse practitioner."

"I already have my eye on one."

"I might have known," Megan said. "How long have you been dating her?"

Torrie laughed. "No dates," she said. "This nurse is also a nun."

"A nun?" Megan asked. "Why would you want to involve a nun?"

Torrie laughed again and held up her hands. "Wait a minute. This has nothing to do with anything but work. I'm not interested in her in any other capacity. I just figured it would be easy to sell a nun on the idea of volunteering her time for the clinic."

"Sounds like a good idea," Megan said. "But how about your love life? Are you seeing anyone special?"

"Not at the moment. I've been too busy." Torrie took a swallow of coffee. "I do plan to ask Erica Christianson to visit for a week this summer." The thought of Erica Christianson's trim, shapely body and strong passionate nature made Torrie's heart beat faster.

"Are you serious about her?" Megan asked.

"I'm serious about wanting to spend a week with her. That's as serious as I get."

"You can't live your whole life just going from one person to another. Sooner or later, you'll have to settle down."

"Says who?" Torrie challenged. "I'm very happy without long-range commitments. I don't think I was meant for anything permanent. The work comes first. Most people don't like that."

"Some day you'll meet someone who will change your mind. Someone you'll want to live with — to grow old with."

"Meggie, I hate to disillusion you, but a permanent relationship just isn't high on my agenda. I like playing the field. I plan to do just that, as long as I can."

"You're hopeless," Megan said. "Lynn and I should just give up on you."

"Well, I'll leave that to you and Lynn. If you find anyone you think will be perfect, give me a call. Or better yet, just send her over." Torrie leaned back in her chair. "Until then, the Erica Christiansons of the world are suiting me just fine. And the nuns who are also registered nurses fill my needs perfectly for staffing a sliding-scale mountain clinic." Torrie smiled. "Far be it from me to mix pleasure and business."

"I think Lynn is probably right about you," Megan said.

"How's that?"

"She says when you do fall in love, it will be head over heels — and for keeps."

"I hate to disagree with a psychiatrist, but if I were Lynn, I wouldn't bet any money on that theory."

"Can I get you more potato salad?" Torrie asked. She took the last bite of her dill pickle. "Another sandwich?"

"No, thank you. I couldn't eat another thing," Diana said. She folded her napkin, placed it beside her plate and picked up the list she had made of Torrie's instructions. "I think I have everything down the way you want them. Winston will be fine."

As if on cue, Winston jumped up on the sofa and crawled into Diana's lap. Torrie watched as Diana rubbed his ears.

"You are such a cutie, Winston," Diana said. "You and I will have a good time together. I'll rub your ears every night. And every night I'll rub your belly and scratch your back."

Torrie saw a side of Diana she had not seen before. Diana wasn't only competent and caring for her patients, she was warm, tender, and didn't mind carrying on a conversation with a two-year-old Yorkshire terrier who was obviously quite taken with her.

"I thought I was the only one who talked to puppies as if they were people," Torrie said. She felt pulled toward Diana's eyes. She's very pretty, Torrie thought. Much too pretty to waste her life as a nun.

Diana put her hands over Winston's ears. "How can you say such things in front of him. You'll hurt his feelings."

"Diana, you are probably the only person in Atlanta who could spoil Winston worse than I have already." Torrie felt great warmth toward Diana. "He won't want you to leave." She leaned back against the sofa. "If I were in his place I'd feel the same way."

"Would you?" Diana looked at her. "Are you saying you'd like your ears and belly rubbed, and your back scratched?" Diana grinned.

"Exactly," Torrie said. "I'm beginning to feel I should send Winston to Baltimore and stay home myself."

Diana laughed and kissed Winston on the top of his head. "We'll both miss you."

"Good, that makes me feel better," Torrie said. "I hope you both miss me something fierce."

Diana met Torrie's eyes. "Not to worry, we already miss you." Diana looked at her watch. "I'd better be going. I have two tests tomorrow."

Torrie picked up Winston and walked Diana to the door. "I really appreciate the favor."

"I appreciate the opportunity," Diana said. "It's sort of like having a family again." She leaned forward and kissed Winston on the head.

Torrie felt the silken softness of Diana's hair as it brushed against her hand. She felt a tightness below and chastised herself for being silly. She hoped her feelings weren't reflected in her face. "Well from here on, consider yourself part of our family. Winston has wanted an aunt for a long time."

"Great," Diana said. "He now has an aunt and a godmother."

"I'm not too sure about the godmother part. He's not Catholic. In fact, he knows very little about organized religion."

Diana patted his head. "Regardless, I can feel a deep sense of spirituality in him." She smiled at Torrie. "Winston and I will discuss it while you're gone."

"Well, thanks again," Torrie said. "I almost forgot your key." She reached into her pocket and handed over the spare. "When I get back, you'll have to fill me in on Winston's progress. In fact let's plan to have dinner at the house when I return. I have a business proposition for you. I feel pretty sure you'll be interested."

"Tell me now," Diana said. "I could use some good news."

"You'll have to wait till I get back. I don't want to take a chance that you'll turn it down because it was presented badly."

"Okay," Diana said. "So I'll see you when you get back. Good luck in Baltimore."

CHAPTER 5

Diana let herself into Torrie's house and was immediately confronted by Winston at his five-pound, barking watchdog best.

"Well you certainly sound fierce," Diana said. She locked the door behind her and bent down to talk to him eye to eye. "You remember me." She held out the back of her hand so he could catch her scent. "That's better," Diana said as Winston licked her hand, then climbed onto Diana's knee and licked her cheek. "Thank you, Winston," Diana said. She held Winston and stood up. "I don't usually get such a warm welcome when I get home from work." She rubbed his ears as she walked into the kitchen. "I wouldn't mind having a Winston of my own when I go to Africa. You're an awful lot of company." He scrambled down. "I think I'll fix us both some supper. How does that sound to you?" She picked up one of Winston's bowls and took a can of dog food from the cupboard. At the sound of the can opener, Winston began to bark and dance about on his hind legs.

"That's right. It's for you, but you must be a gentleman and wait for me."

She fixed herself a sandwich, and Winston followed her into the family room and began eating as soon as she placed his bowl on the floor next to the sofa.

She selected a novel from Torrie's bookcase and sat down to eat her turkey sandwich and read. It was, for her, the most peaceful hour a day.

She opened *The Thornbirds* and had read the first two sentences when something white and rectangular fell out of the book and onto the soft white carpet.

She picked up a white envelope and three photographs. The woman in the photos caught her attention. She looked closely at the two women standing arm in arm in front of a ski lift. Diana recognized Torrie immediately. She was laughing and brushing snow from her face. The woman at her side was shorter, with blonde hair and blue eyes that seemed fastened on Torrie with unadulterated admiration.

How did Torrie find time for a ski trip? She always seemed completely consumed by her work. On the back of one photo, the handwriting was clear and in ink. Diana glanced at the inscription. "Words pale in the light of memory. I will remember always."

Suddenly her heart begin to race. How did it feel to have someone care about you that much? she wondered. Somehow, she wasn't surprised to see another woman in the photos. She put back *The Thornbirds* in its original position, running her fingertips over the bindings of the books on either side. What other secrets were hidden inside these covers? A card, a letter, other photographs ... meant only for Torrie's fiery green eyes, meant only for Torrie's understanding, only for Torrie's heart. But Diana had seen, her mind had imagined, and her heart understood more than she would ever have asked.

Her heart beat faster. Why should any of this matter to her? Her life was not entwined with Torrie's. Even the thought was ridiculous.

Just because Torrie knows a lot of women, she told herself, doesn't mean there's something abnormal about her relationships. A lot of career women were different. So what? Nuns were different too. Maybe she'd bring the subject up when Torrie returned from Johns Hopkins. It wasn't really any of her business unless Torrie chose to share those secrets with her.

She felt the softness of Winston's fur as he jumped up on the sofa and climbed into her lap. Diana patted his head. "You're just in time for evening prayers," Diana told him. She pulled a small prayer book from her pocket, and she began to recite the vespers, feeling warm, comforted, and safe.

CHAPTER 6

"Where is everybody?" Torrie called as she closed the front door behind her. In less than five seconds, Winston scampered into the hallway and headed straight for her. Diana appeared right behind him.

Torrie picked Winston up and laughed as he licked her face. She looked at Diana and smiled. It was nice to come back to a house with someone waiting in it.

"It's usually lonely coming home from a trip," she said. "I really appreciate your staying with him."

"It was fun," Diana said. "Besides, it gave me a

break in the battle over my lease. They want a fortune for the apartment I'm renting. I'm still trying to find a place I can afford."

"It's a month-to-month lease?" Torrie asked as they went to the kitchen and she poured herself a cup of coffee.

Diana nodded.

Torrie felt a tingle of excitement. "Diana, I have an idea. Why don't you move in here? You can have the full run of the house, and there's enough space for privacy. Plus, you'd be doing me a big favor since I have to be out of town at least one weekend a month. Knowing you're here to look after Winston would make me feel a lot better. In exchange, whatever you're paying in rent, I'll cut in half." She stopped, trying to gauge Diana's reaction.

"That wouldn't be fair to you," Diana said slowly. "Besides, you're not used to having someone around all the time. It might get on your nerves after a while."

"We're only talking about three months or so." Torrie shrugged. "Didn't you say you were going back to Africa a week or two after graduation?" They took their coffee into the den and sat down on the sofa. She looked at Diana. "You'd never get a lease on any place decent for just three months. Besides, I've already paid out a fortune to Winston's regular house sitter, and she's only here with him for two hours a day." Torrie smiled. "Winston and I both want you to stay. Please say yes."

Diana returned the smile. "How can I refuse? Of course, I'll stay, but it's you who's doing me the favor."

"I think we're all getting something good out of

the arrangement," Torrie said. "And that includes Winston."

They discussed the details and she agreed to help Diana move her things in at the end of the week.

"So," Diana said. "Tell me what you learned at Johns Hopkins."

"According to Doctor Kirkland, there are about fifteen allergens in various combinations that are triggering the headaches — including Winston." Torrie kissed Winston on the head.

"How awful! Will you have to give him away?"

"Not on your life! I can live with the headaches, but I'm not too sure how well I'd do if I had to turn Winston over to strangers." She scratched Winston behind the ears. "Kirkland is mailing a serum to me next week. The injections should neutralize the effects of most of the allergens — including Winston. But in any event, Winston stays."

"Somehow I felt sure he would," Diana said. "And thank you again for inviting me to share your home."

"Thank you for accepting," Torrie said. She has beautiful eyes, she thought. "Winston and I feel better already."

CHAPTER 7

The weeks flew by as Diana threw herself into her work at the hospital. The internship demanded a lot of her time, but now that she was settled in at Torrie's, she had developed a routine that suited her.

She and Torrie spent one or two evenings a week together, usually talking about medicine, their hopes for the future, and their childhood memories. Each evening spent in Torrie's company left Diana looking forward to the next, with greater anticipation.

She was happy, she realized as she watched Torrie rearrange the logs in the fireplace, set down the poker, and replace the fire screen. Orange and yellow flames shot upward like outstretched hands reaching for a prize of great value. What was it in people and fire that could not refrain from reaching beyond itself, and finding nothing, could not refrain from reaching out again?

"You look as if you're light-years away. What are you thinking about so seriously?" Torrie asked.

In the dimly lit room, Torrie was bathed in shadows and fire-light. Waves of light danced across her eyes and mouth, bathing them in warmth. Broad bands of darkness concealed Torrie's breasts and thighs. Bright red and yellow flames outlined Torrie's head and shoulders, like solar flares shot upward by her thoughts.

"Are you going to tell me or is it a secret?"

Torrie's eyes were burning jade.

Diana felt something inside her reaching out to Torrie, yet falling short of contact. "I was thinking how fire and the human soul are so much alike."

"How's that?" Torrie crossed the room, carrying the fire in her eyes, and sat down next to her.

"Both give warmth and light to life. Both attract like a magnet. Both recreate themselves constantly."

"What makes you so sure there is a soul?" Torrie asked. "I've seen every part of the human body, inside and out, and I've never seen the soul."

Diana laughed. "How strange. I can't look at you without seeing the soul, and you don't see it even when you look."

"We're very different kinds of people. We see the world through different windows. You look for life after death; I've seen enough death to know that you'd better do your living here and now."

"I'm certainly not against living," Diana said. "Life is a gift meant to be lived. I simply believe that we survive death: that we're immortal. It would be a terrible injustice if we didn't."

"Yeah, well, life is filled with injustice. Surely your convent walls haven't blocked your view of the truth." Torrie's tone was edged with a sarcasm that caught Diana by surprise.

"Is that your impression of me? That I close my eyes to reality?" Diana was hurt. "I thought you knew me better than that."

"There's a part of you I don't know at all." Firelight moved against Torrie's cheek. "I can't figure out why someone as bright as you became a nun. You could teach on the faculty of any nursing school in this country. Any of them would be lucky to have you. You could have your work and a full life."

"My life is full, and I don't want to teach in a nursing school. I like my life."

"Compared to what? Do you even know what you've given up? Haven't you ever wondered what it would be like to love someone and express that love physically, what it's like to be loved in return?" Torrie took a deep breath. "What ever possessed you to become a nun?"

Torrie's questions were like quick sharp jabs delivered in a boxing ring. Her mind reeled. Questions she never expected to hear were being delivered by an opponent she had never expected to face. She struggled to regain her emotional footing and to force her scattered thoughts into some kind of order. She wanted to deliver answers that possessed the sharpness and clarity of truth.

"I can't remember a time when I didn't want to

be a nun. I grew up in a family that saw the church as the center of their life. They were very disappointed when my brother didn't become a priest." Diana paused, remembering her parents' heated conversations. "They were surprised when I told them that I wanted to be a nun. Gradually they accepted my vocation, almost as a consolation prize. It wasn't as good as a son becoming a priest, but it was better than not having any of your children become a 'religious.' "

"That must have made you feel awful," Torrie said.

"It did, but I never really told them how I felt. I just waited, hoping they'd come to value my choice more as time passed."

"And did they?"

"Yes." Diana felt the sadness that she had carried inside her for years. "They eventually claimed it as something they were proud of. Now they stand on the fact that their daughter is a nun. In a way, it puts them on a pedestal in their neighborhood. They live in a kind of reflected glory."

"But what made you want to be a nun in the first place?"

Images of her childhood played across Diana's mind: her first communion at age seven; her weekly confessions of childhood sins; her rote recitation of prescribed prayers; her confirmation at age eleven; her daily meditations; her mental conversations with God.

"I fell in love with God while I was still a child." She watched Torrie's face for signs of recognition or disbelief. "He was the one person I could always count on, the one person who always understood.

Prayer and meditation became more and more rewarding for me, and I spent more and more time practicing both." Diana recognized an irony in what she was saying and shrugged. "I guess it was a lot like addiction. The more I meditated, the more I wanted to meditate; the more I felt comforted, the more comfort I sought." She met Torrie's eyes directly. "Keeping company with God can be very addictive. I got hooked at an early age. Hooked in a positive sense. The more I knew God, the more I wanted to know Him better. It must be very much like falling in love with a person. The deeper I fell, the deeper I wanted to fall. The attraction to God gets stronger as one gets closer to Him."

"You never felt attracted to a real person?" Torrie's expression was a mixture of surprise and curiosity.

Diana laughed. "To me, God is a real person. But I know what you mean. No, I've never been attracted in a romantic or sexual way to men. It all seems perfectly natural to me — being in love with God. I can't really imagine anything else. I'm totally committed to God and my vows."

"Don't you miss a sexual relationship? Surely that's one place where God would be a less than adequate stand-in."

"I've never been involved sexually, so I don't have a comparison."

"You've never . . . not even in nursing school?" Torrie's expression was incredulous.

"I went to nursing school after I entered the convent," Diana said. "I lived with the sisters, not in the dorms. So sex wasn't even a question. In fact, my vow of chastity has always been easy for me because I've never been tempted."

"You don't know what you've missed." Torrie's words sounded like a statement of fact rather than a judgment.

"I could say the same thing to you, you know, about the spiritual side of life." Emboldened, she went on. "In fact, I'd be willing to bet that outside of your work, you've never really been committed to anyone."

"And you'd win the bet," Torrie said. "I have never been tempted to make commitments outside of my work. I consider that a blessing. My life is uncomplicated because I don't have to choose between a commitment to work and a commitment to a person. I've seen a lot of people who are miserable because they're trying to juggle two or more commitments in their lives. I like my life exactly as it is — simple and without personal commitments."

"We're not so unlike each other after all," Diana said. "I like my life just the way it is, too." She felt a new surge of confidence. "Neither of us wants a commitment to an individual person. Unlike most people, I don't choose to move from relationship to relationship, leaving before any real connections are established. My vow of chastity spares me that indignity." Diana stopped, knowing that this time it was she who threw the punch, and Torrie who looked stunned.

"You shouldn't make judgments about things you know nothing about," Torrie snapped.

"Nor should you." Diana shot back.

"Touché!" Torrie said. "Let's just call it a draw and drop the subject."

Diana was embarrassed. Since when did a nun engage in a battle out of anger, or label a friend an adversary? The stark reality of the exchange made her feel numb. She owed Torrie an apology — didn't she? Was there any question? Yet, some fierce un-nun-like thing deep inside her resisted even the hint of an apology. She forced herself to say what she could to heal the wounds each had inflicted on the other.

"You're right," Diana said. "Let's drop the subject." She extended her hand. "Friends?"

"Friends." Torrie's hand closed around hers and Diana was keenly aware of the warm, silken softness of Torrie's skin.

CHAPTER 8

Between her headache and her concern over the conversation she had had with Diana earlier in the evening, Torrie felt too tense to sleep.

She reached for the bedside lamp, switched it on and looked at the clock. One-fifteen. She swallowed one tablet of Tylenol and Codeine with cold water from a thermal mug.

She closed her eyes and immediately saw Diana as she had been only an hour before — defiant, angry, and straining to maintain her composure. She shouldn't have pushed her so hard about why she had entered the convent. It was really none of her business. Why couldn't she just forget about her as anything but a nurse practitioner? In two months she'd be on her way to Africa. They'd probably never see each other again.

Sadness descended like a heavy curtain cutting her off from the world. She tried to tell herself that once Diana was gone, things would get back to normal, but the image of Diana refused to go away. Torrie felt her stomach tighten and her heartbeat quicken. She imagined leaning forward and kissing Diana lightly on the mouth. Diana's mouth would open to receive her . . . She shivered as the tightness below grew more intense.

"No!" She sat bolt upright in the bed. She couldn't feel like this about a nun. It was absolutely crazy! There were plenty of gay women out there who were better-looking and professionally established. Why was she lying awake thinking about kissing someone whose idea of a romantic date was attending mass or meditating about the nature of God? She leaned back against her pillow. She had to get away for a while. Anything to take her mind off Diana. She could spend a few days with Erica Christianson, she mused. That would take her mind off Diana.

She looked at the clock again. She could call Erica, leave Diana a note, and fly to Nashville first thing in the morning. She'd call Jim Baldwin and get him to cover for her. She reached for the phone. She needed to forget Diana. She would not fall in love with anyone — least of all, a nun.

A sleepy voice answered the phone on the fourth ring. "Hello, Doctor Christianson here."

"Erica, this is Torrie. I'm sorry to call you so late, but I'm thinking of coming to Nashville in the morning and wondered if I could stay at your place."

"Torrie Lassiter." Erica no longer sounded sleepy. "You'd better stay with me. In fact, I'm off tomorrow so get here early. I'll fix you breakfast in bed."

CHAPTER 9

Diana had been listening for Torrie's car for an hour. "I don't understand it, Winston." She rubbed the dog's ears and leaned back against the sofa cushions. "Your mother should have been here by now. She must have stopped somewhere. I hope she hasn't eaten — that would spoil our surprise dinner." She looked at her watch. "If she's not here soon, she's going to have overdone turkey and cold mashed potatoes."

Winston jumped to his feet, his ears erect, and looked toward the door.

"Is that her, boy?" Diana heard the sound of a key click in the door and felt her heart beat faster. Winston ran down the hall and Diana followed. She smiled as she saw Torrie and stopped short when she saw another woman behind her.

Torrie bent down and scooped Winston up in her arms. "Did you miss me?" She spoke directly to the dog. "I missed you." She looked up and saw Diana. "Diana, I wasn't sure you'd be here." She nodded toward the tall, blonde, attractive woman next to her. "Diana Colletti, this is Erica Christianson. Erica's a resident in cardiology at Vanderbilt. She'll be staying here overnight. She's going to a cardiology seminar at the Hilton in the morning."

"Hi." Erica extended her hand. "Torrie told me you're a nun, and you'll be going to Africa in a couple of months. That sounds fascinating. I'd love to hear more about your work there."

Diana felt heartsick. The whole evening was ruined, she thought. Why didn't Torrie tell her that she'd be bringing someone home with her? Diana stepped forward and shook Erica's hand.

"It's nice to meet you. You're just in time for dinner. I'll just set one more place and check on the turkey."

"I thought I smelled turkey," Torrie said. "What a surprise! We're both starving. We were in such a hurry to get here that we didn't stop to eat."

"In that case, we can eat in about fifteen minutes." Diana forced a smile. "You two relax and I'll call you when dinner's ready."

"Thanks." Torrie turned toward Erica. "I'll take your bag upstairs. Make yourself comfortable."

Diana returned to the kitchen, turned the oven

off and removed the fifteen-pound turkey she had prepared for Torrie's welcome home.

Why did she invite her, Diana asked herself as she placed a spoon in the cranberry sauce.

"What can I do to help?" The unfamiliar voice startled her. She turned to see Erica standing in the doorway. "I'm pretty good in the kitchen. Just give me my orders."

"That was a great dinner, Diana." Torrie placed the tray of coffee on the cocktail table and sat down next to Erica on the sofa.

"Thanks." Diana watched as Torrie handed Erica a cup of coffee.

"One sugar," Torrie said as Erica took the cup from her hand. Erica's hand seemed to rest on Torrie's for a second or two more than necessary, and Diana felt an overpowering desire to push Erica from the sofa and reclaim the place where she had sat with Torrie over the past month.

"Torrie seems to think that you're not well advised about your options right here in Georgia, that your going to Africa is a mistake for someone so talented," Erica said.

Diana felt the blood pounding in her temples. How dare Torrie discuss her personal plans with a stranger. Torrie had no right or permission to discuss her affairs with anyone. It took every bit of control she could muster not to tell them both what she thought of them.

"Torrie has a little trouble accepting the fact that nuns take orders from their superiors. We can't just decide we'd rather work somewhere else."

"Does that mean you can't work at the clinic in Saint Cloud?" Erica asked.

Diana looked at Torrie. "I'm afraid I know nothing about the clinic. Torrie hasn't mentioned it to me."

"I've been meaning to," Torrie said.

"Well, now is as good a time as any." Erica placed her hand on Torrie's arm.

Diana wanted to get up and leave the room, but she forced herself to sit and listen to Torrie discuss things she had thought were private.

"The clinic will be opening in about three weeks. It will operate on a sliding-scale basis. Mark and I will donate our services. We could use a good nurse practitioner. It would just about double the people we'd be able to treat. Mark and I would really like to have you as our nurse practitioner. We couldn't pay you as much as you'd make in a regular clinic, but the rewards in personal satisfaction would outdo any high-paying clinic." Torrie smiled. "We really do need you, Diana. I hope you'll consider it seriously."

"I'll help however I can," she replied, "but I'll be leaving soon. You couldn't count on me for very long."

"We'll take you for however long you can stay." Torrie sounded happy. "Who knows, the job may grow on you."

"I wouldn't count on me for the long haul. When I graduate, I'll be on my way to Africa." Diana stood up. "And if I want to graduate on schedule, I'd better get my assignment read. So I'll say good night."

"That's fine. I'm tired myself," Torrie said. "I think it's time we turned in too. Erica's seminar starts at ten sharp. Why don't we all go to breakfast at the Original Pancake House at eight o'clock? That would give us time for a leisurely breakfast together."

"That sounds fine," Erica said. "How about it, Diana?"

"Sure," Diana said. "That would be great."

"Good. It's settled," Torrie said.

Moments later, Diana watched as Erica and Torrie climbed the stairs. She wanted to shout, "Don't take her to your bedroom." Instead she spoke in a calm voice. "Sleep well."

CHAPTER 10

By seven the next morning, Diana had made a pot of coffee, retrieved the Sunday paper from the front porch and was waiting in the den for Torrie and Erica. She skimmed the front page and tried to keep her mind off Torrie and Erica.

Diana had fed Winston and finished two cups of coffee and the entire Sunday paper before she decided to take Winston for a short walk. When they returned twenty minutes later, Diana could scarcely believe that Torrie and her guest were still upstairs.

Two hours later, Torrie and Erica finally appeared. Diana was furious. It took a heroic effort not to attack them verbally. She couldn't take her eyes off Torrie, and she wondered if Torrie could see the anger that burned behind them. She wanted Torrie to know that she considered her actions incredibly rude and thoughtless. How could she bring a woman home with her to spend the night? How could they plan to go to breakfast with her and then not show up? She wouldn't be as rude as they had been. She would keep her dignity.

"Good morning," Torrie said. "I hope you slept well."

"Very well, thank you," Diana said. "I doubt that we have time to get breakfast before your seminar."

"I'm afraid I'm running late," Erica said. "I'll have to get something at the hotel before the seminar starts."

Diana fought to maintain her composure.

"Do you need me to lead you to the expressway?" Torrie asked.

"No, thanks. I remember the way from my last visit," Erica said. She winked at Torrie, and Diana felt the heat rising up her neck and into her temples. "Thanks for putting me up for the night. You saved a poor resident a hundred and fifty dollars." She leaned forward and kissed Torrie on the cheek. "Call me when you plan to be in Nashville again. I'll buy you dinner."

Diana could feel the blood pounding in her ears. Why doesn't she just leave, Diana thought. She had already ruined last night's dinner, and now this morning's breakfast.

"I'll walk you to your car." Torrie glanced at Diana. "If you'd like, I'll take you to brunch."

Diana struggled to control her anger. "That would be nice," she said.

The door closed behind the two women.

"What in the world is the matter with me?" she said in a low voice. She hugged a sofa pillow to herself. She couldn't live like this, she thought. God, what was she saying? Why should she care who Torrie had for an overnight guest? Overnight guest, my foot! Who Torrie was sleeping with, was more like it. Was she being too much of a nun? After all, Torrie's lifestyle was her own business. Maybe she shouldn't say anything. She didn't want to end up sounding jealous when in fact she was merely interested in the welfare of her soul.

She heard the door close and Torrie flopped down in a chair across from her.

"Erica can't get over me sharing a house with a nun," Torrie said. "I guess it does sound weird to anyone who's known me for a while."

Diana's stomach was churning, her heart was racing and her temples were pounding. That's it, she thought. How dare the two of them discuss her. For a moment her control slipped, and Diana could hear herself saying things she felt sure were better left unsaid.

"I've been thinking about moving anyway. Now is as good a time as any. I'm sorry I make you feel weird. I thought we had a pretty decent friendship."

Torrie looked stunned. "Who said anything about you moving? I like your living here. I'd miss you if you left, and so would Winston."

Diana could feel the warm wetness of tears on her cheeks. "I can't live here anymore, Torrie. I have to move."

She didn't see Torrie get up, but the next moment, Torrie was kneeling in front of her and had taken hold of her hand. Torrie's skin was soft and warm.

"Please tell me what's wrong, Diana." Torrie's voice was filled with sincerity. "I've never seen you so upset. Have I offended you in some way? I wouldn't do that knowingly. I really care about you. Please talk to me, Diana. I don't want you to go."

Diana looked into Torrie's green eyes and wished she could crawl inside them. She felt certain she would find safety there.

"Tell me, what's upset you so?" Torrie's voice was pleading.

Diana felt overcome with emotion. Her mind recalled the old-fashioned paperweight on the desk in her bedroom. She could see it clearly, but now Torrie and she were the tiny figures inside the glass bubble, and forces beyond her control had turned the globe over, shaken it, and set it right side up again. A blizzard of thoughts and emotions were swirling around them, blocking her clear view of Torrie, making her seek physical contact for assurance. She clasped Torrie's hand firmly between her own.

"I can't stay here anymore. I've stayed too long already. I need to leave Atlanta." Panic rose in her as she spoke.

"Has your order complained about your being here?" Torrie asked. "Did someone say something about your living in my house? If they have, let me talk to them. I'm sure I can convince them that you're in no danger here. Even nuns need friends. I consider you a very dear friend."

Before last night such a statement might have comforted her, but it was too late for such declarations. Diana took a deep breath and looked directly into Torrie's eyes.

"It's not that simple, Torrie. I feel more for you than friendship, and the very idea scares me to death! I've no right to have such feelings. I'm a nun. I'm certainly not a . . . a . . . lesbian. No matter how I feel about you, I'm not a lesbian." Diana felt the heat in her face and knew she was blushing.

"How do you feel about me, Diana?" Torrie brushed the tears from Diana's cheeks.

"I don't even know how to express it." Diana felt embarrassed and relieved at the same time. "I want to touch you . . . to feel your body against mine." Diana closed her eyes as if to hide from the truth. "I was so jealous of Erica that I couldn't even sleep last night. I can't bear to think of you two together." Diana looked at Torrie through tear-filled eyes. "I'm so sorry, Torrie. I know this must make you uncomfortable. I'll ask the mother house to transfer me to another state."

"Please don't do that, Diana." Torrie's voice was soft and calm. "I've been over and over this with myself. I'm very attracted to you, but I wouldn't do anything that would hurt you." Torrie trailed the back of her hand lightly over Diana's face. "I've wanted to take you into my arms more times than I can count. I've stopped myself from kissing you at least twice a day." She smiled. "I think I'm falling in love with you, and I want more than a visitor's day with you each month."

Diana threw her arms around Torrie and rested her cheek against Torrie's face. "This whole thing is ridiculous. You don't even want a commitment, and my commitment was made before I even knew you existed. The only thing we could mean to each other, in any way but friendship, is grief." She pulled back and looked at Torrie. "I don't ever want to feel again the jealousy and anger I felt this morning. You hadn't done me any wrong, and yet I wanted to hit you."

"Did you?" Torrie asked softly. "I wanted to do this." She raised Diana's chin, leaned forward and kissed her gently on the mouth.

Diana's heart raced as the softness of Torrie's lips brushed against her own. For an instant, she yielded completely to the fires that Torrie's kiss had started inside her. She wrapped her arms around Torrie and drew her close. Her lips parted to the gentle touch of Torrie's tongue. The stark white heat of desire flowed like molten lava through Diana's veins and started new fires of passion in her heart. Suddenly her world had become a single desire. Diana wanted Torrie. The thought formed in her mind like smoke rising from a roaring fire. It hung suspended at the edges of her awareness. Suddenly, in the space between two heartbeats, another thought crashed into her con- sciousness. The recognition of her desire struck terror in her soul. She released Torrie and pulled backward, out of her embrace.

"No! I can't do this!" Diana was talking more to herself than to Torrie. "I've taken vows. I can't want you. I can't!" She could feel tears streaming down her face, feel herself on the edge of panic.

"Diana, it's all right." Torrie's voice was calm and strong. "I shouldn't have kissed you. I should have known better. It's all my fault and it won't happen again," Torrie said. "I give you my word."

Diana's panic lessened as she recognized the consternation in Torrie's face. "Please accept my apology," Torrie said.

Diana wanted to reassure her. She wanted to tell her everything would be all right, but she knew that would be a lie. Everything would not be all right. Nothing would ever be the same again. She had broken her vows in her heart, and nothing would change that fact. She was more at fault for yielding than Torrie was for initiating the kiss.

"You don't owe me an apology," Diana said. "In fact, I probably owe you one. I allowed it to happen. I should have been stronger. What I did could have ruined our friendship."

"Diana, please don't throw our friendship away for a single mistake. I don't want to lose you as a friend." Torrie's voice shook with emotion.

Diana clasped Torrie's hand. "I won't give up our friendship." She inhaled deeply. "But I'm not sure I can live here any longer."

Torrie's face turned pale. "Please don't move out because of this. It was just one kiss. It won't happen again."

"It wasn't just one kiss." Diana was determined to be as honest as possible. "I kissed you back. I enjoyed it. And — I wanted you physically." Diana managed a smile. "For a nun who's already taken her vows, that's a lot more than one kiss."

"Surely you don't think I'd push myself on you." Torrie sounded distressed.

Diana squeezed Torrie's hand. "Of course not. I know you'd never hurt me. But it's not you I worry about. It's me. What just happened is so foreign to me that if anyone had predicted it, I would have thought them insane. I'm the weak one."

"Well, I won't let it happen again. I can be strong enough for both of us." Torrie's eyes showed great resolve.

"You're wonderfully sweet and gentle, but I'm going to need a little more reinforcement than you can give me," Diana said, smiling. "I'm scheduled for a religious retreat at the mother house next week. I think I'll call and change it to this week. I need time to think, to align my priorities."

"And will you come back when the week is finished?" Torrie asked.

"I will if I'm sure I can honor my vows and have a friendship with you at the same time."

"You can, Diana," Torrie said. "I know you can. You have to give me another chance. We can be very good friends without dishonoring your vows or our friendship."

Diana wanted to believe her, but she didn't know how serious that one kiss was.

"I'll come back," Diana said. "If only to tell you in person what I've decided."

"When would you leave?" Torrie asked.

"If they agree, tomorrow morning. On the earliest flight I can get."

"What about your classes?"

"I'll make them up — if you'll allow that," Diana said.

"Just come back, Diana, and we'll work out everything."

CHAPTER 11

Torrie had already spent three miserable days wondering what Diana would decide, and it was only Tuesday. At a time when Torrie hoped to be kept busy, the hospital was unusually quiet, allowing her more time to speculate on the outcome of Diana's religious retreat.

Torrie decided early Tuesday morning that she would invite Lynn Bradley to dinner and get the benefit of her advice concerning what had happened with Diana. When Lynn arrived, Torrie was waiting with a bottle of white zinfandel and a plate of hors d'oeuvres.

"You look as nervous as some of my patients on the locked wards," Lynn said, handing her jacket to Torrie. She popped a shrimp into her mouth and helped herself to the wine. "So why don't you tell Mother Lynn what's bothering you."

Torrie filled her in on everything that had happened since she met Diana.

"You know, Torrie," Lynn said, "I think you're getting a bit balmy as you get older. Who the hell in her right mind tries to seduce a nun? If you're looking for a challenge, try research." She took a sip of wine and looked Torrie in the eyes. "As a lapsed Catholic, I can tell you that anything involving nuns is bound to be a problem. They start out with two strikes against them. One, they're goofy enough to give up sex, and two, they really believe they're married to God." Lynn leaned toward Torrie and patted her on the thigh. "Find yourself a nice Presbyterian, or an Episcopalian. They don't get so involved with their religion."

"I'm not trying to find a nice anything," Torrie said. "I just don't want Diana to move away because of one kiss."

"Why not? You've often said that you don't want commitments. What could an affair with her lead to except trouble? She'd end up out of the convent, or feeling guiltier than hell, or both." Lynn shrugged. "Face the facts, Torrie, you have nothing to offer this woman. Anybody willing to take lifelong vows of poverty, chastity and obedience is going to expect a commitment — in any kind of relationship. You're just not the type to make that kind of commitment."

Torrie was insulted. "Maybe I've changed. Maybe I really care about her." Torrie wondered if Lynn saw it too — the possibility of change in her. "You told me once that if I ever made a lifetime commitment to anybody, it would be to a 'unique individual.' "

Lynn's eyes opened wide with surprise and amusement. "My use of that term, 'unique individual,' didn't cover nuns. That's a little *too* unique, even for you. What I had in mind was a woman who would pretty much let you do as you pleased, in exchange for a commitment to live together and grow old together."

"Are you saying that I'm incapable of real commitment?" Torrie felt herself slip past annoyance into anger.

"I seem to remember you telling me that once," Lynn said softly, her face kind. "Have you changed, Torrie? Or are you kidding yourself for a few hours of a guilt-free conscience?"

Torrie had had all of Lynn's bluntness she intended to take for one evening. "Just because you were my psychiatrist five years ago doesn't mean you know me, inside and out, today."

Lynn put her wine glass down and folded her arms. "Torrie, I'm not trying to be your psychiatrist. I'm your friend. We've shared too much truth to begin to lie to each other now." She uncrossed her arms and took hold of Torrie's hand. "If you feel you want to make a commitment to this nun —"

"Diana. Her name is Diana."

Lynn shook her head. "All right then, if you feel you want to make a commitment to Diana, it means you've had a major change in your attitude concerning relationships. But in this case, your change in attitude might not be enough for a relationship. A nun makes some pretty serious promises to God and her order. It's not likely she'll toss them aside because of one kiss."

"That's not what really bothers me." Torrie knew she always got the truth from Lynn. She wanted the truth now, no matter how painful it might be. "What I want to know is, do you think she'll toss our friendship away because of one kiss? I've kicked myself a hundred times for kissing her. I should have known better."

"Kicking yourself won't change anything." Lynn reached for her wine glass. "Whether or not she leaves your house depends mainly on what she feels for you already. If you've become important enough for her to risk breaking her vows again, then her feelings for you have already put her career in jeopardy. Nuns aren't supposed to covet men; to covet a woman would be much more serious." Lynn took a deep breath. "I think it's imperative that you sort through your own feelings and decide exactly what you want from her, and what you're willing to give in exchange for it. Figure that out and you're way ahead of the game."

Instinctively Torrie knew that Lynn was right. No matter what Diana ended up doing, Torrie had to make her own choices — hopefully before Diana returned.

She smiled at Lynn. "You've earned your fee, Doctor."

"Somehow, knowing that makes me feel like my day has been worthwhile. And you know what my price is for professional advice."

Torrie shook her head and laughed. "How could I forget? A free coronary bypass, with me assisting Meggie, should you ever need one."

"Right," Lynn said. "And plastic surgery for the scar!"

"You've got it!" Torrie said. "But I hope I never have to pay off."

"You and me both, Doc," Lynn said. "You and me both."

CHAPTER 12

Diana's first three days at the mother house were spent in complete silence, and almost total isolation.

Her days and nights were filled with meditation, silent prayer, long walks, and thoughts of Torrie. Nothing — not the ritual of the daily office, not the discipline of twice-daily meditations, and not the almost total fast she had observed since her arrival had taken her mind off Torrie.

Torrie's kiss had somehow become part of her. Its touch lingered on her lips; its taste filled her mouth and invaded her awareness. The hundreds of miles she had put between herself and Torrie had done little to wipe Torrie from her mind.

What was it Father O'Keefe had told her in the confessional? Oh, yes, Diana remembered. "Treat this doctor as you would any temptation which has the power to drag your soul into hell. Face it, and beat it."

Father O'Keefe had clearly never encountered a temptation as strong as Torrie. It was easy to renounce things you'd never known, she thought. It certainly couldn't be considered informed consent.

Diana looked at the tabernacle on the main altar. *Why don't you comfort me now, Lord? Why don't you take away these memories that disturb my concentration and my peace? If my attraction to Torrie goes against your will, then, I beg of you, remove the attraction.*

There was a light tap on her shoulder, and Diana turned to look into the small withered face of Sister Josephine. The nun pointed to the door and indicated that Diana was to follow her out of the chapel.

Once outside, Sister Josephine whispered, "You have guests in the East Parlor. Your parents are here."

"My parents?" Diana felt as if someone had hit her in the stomach. Why now, she wondered. She had enough to work out without having to deal with their view on how great it was that she was a nun.

"Yes. Mother General has given you special permission to visit with them." The withered face wrinkled into a smile. "The community is very proud of your work in Africa. We're also aware that, in a matter of weeks, you'll be returning there." The ancient nun stopped outside the doors of the East Parlor. "Have a pleasant visit," she said, then shuffled off down the long, narrow hallway.

Diana took a deep breath and exhaled forcefully, then stepped into the large, antique-filled parlor and was nearly knocked off balance by the force of her parents embrace.

"You look so thin," her mother said. "Have you been ill?"

"Your mother's right, Diana. You could use another ten or fifteen pounds."

"Honestly, you two would say that no matter how much I weighed." She sat down between them, held their hands and asked, "How have you two been? How're the boys?"

"They're fine. Peter is being transferred to Fort Benning in two weeks. He's been promoted to major," her mother said. "He looks so handsome in his uniform."

"Not as handsome as he would have looked in a Roman collar, or vestments for mass," her father chimed in. "Peter should have been a priest."

"Now, Dad, there's no use going over that again," Diana said. "Peter didn't feel called to the priesthood. He's a good Army officer."

"Diana's right, Joe, we're blessed to have our daughter as a nun, a missionary."

"Of course we are." He squeezed his daughter's hand. "We're very proud of you."

"We also want to know why you didn't tell us you were coming to the mother house. We found out by accident from Sister Robert." Her voice had a singsong rhythm Diana found irritating. "I could have baked a cake if I had known you'd be here."

"Mother, we get so much cake and sweets here . . ."

"When are you going back to Africa?" her father boomed.

"About a month after I finish my training," Diana said. She wouldn't see Torrie for years. The thought surprised her with a sadness she hadn't expected.

"Peter plans to take you to dinner when he gets to Atlanta. Your father and I are planning to visit you both in Atlanta before you have to leave."

The idea sent chills through Diana. She had no desire to have her parents meet Torrie.

When the visiting hour was over, Diana walked her parents to the main door and kissed them good-bye.

"I almost forgot." Her mother was digging into her overstuffed pocketbook. "Here it is." She unfolded two sheets of yellow legal paper. "It's the neighborhood prayer list." She pointed to number eight — Katherine Scalia. "I'm not sure prayer is what's called for here. Anyway, Mrs. Scalia asks that you pray Katherine gets married before she gets pregnant." She pursed her lips. "It would be a shame . . . so maybe you can pray for Mrs. Scalia. Maybe you can help her." She patted Diana's shoulder. "But what do I know? You're the professional."

Diana nodded assent and watched her parents walk out the front door. She crossed herself, as if beginning or ending a prayer, then sighed.

What would it be like to have to explain her feelings for Torrie to her parents? Better to be torn apart by lions, she thought. Her parents would never understand.

CHAPTER 13

Torrie looked out the window for the sixth time, hoping to see Diana getting out of a cab. She checked her watch. It had been more than thirty minutes. There should have been plenty of taxis at the airport. She stopped pacing and took a deep breath.

Calm down, she told herself, you need to be calm when Diana gets here.

She would listen calmly and accept her decision, no matter what it was. She took another deep breath and went to make a pot of coffee.

Ten minutes later, the doorbell rang and Torrie started toward the door.

Don't hug her unless she hugs you first, Torrie told herself. Don't act too excited to see her. And don't kiss her — not even on the cheek.

Her heart beat faster as she saw Diana standing on the front steps holding her small black leather suitcase. "Let me help you." She took Diana's bag and led her into the den. "Coffee or tea?"

"Maybe later," Diana said.

A fur-covered blur shot out of the kitchen and headed straight for Diana. With one leap, all four feet left the floor and Winston landed in Diana's lap. A moment later, he was covering Diana's face with kisses.

Torrie smiled as she watched them. "He's awfully happy to have you home. We both are."

Winston's body shook with excitement as he continued to lick Diana's face and ears.

"What a welcome!" Diana said, hugging Winston and scratching him behind the ears.

"How was your retreat?" Torrie steeled herself for an answer she didn't want to hear.

"It went pretty well. It helped me put my thoughts and feelings in order."

"And?" She was braced for the worst.

Diana looked directly at her and spoke in a soft and steady voice. "I know for sure that I don't want to lose you as a friend. And I know that there must never be any kind of physical contact between us again." She quickly added, "Not that I don't find you attractive. I do." Her face flushed a deep red. "I feel disassociated when I hear myself say things like that. It's as if someone else were speaking through me."

Diana cleared her throat and continued. "I tried to figure out why I feel the way I do about you, why I'm attracted to you, but I'm no closer to understanding my feelings than I was a week ago. I've resigned myself to resisting the temptation, just as I would any other." She looked into Torrie's eyes, and Torrie remembered the softness of Diana's mouth against her own. "Besides, in a matter of weeks, I'll be back in Africa and the question of my feelings won't matter one bit."

Torrie felt relieved and sick at the same time. Diana was attracted to her. That was good. But she'd soon be out of the country, and that was not good. Or was it? Lynn Bradley would say it was good, but what did Lynn know?

"I wish you'd say something, Torrie. Do you still want me to stay, or have you changed your mind?"

Torrie's thoughts swirled like leaves caught in a hurricane. Not want her to stay? Impossible. But why, Torrie asked herself for the hundredth time, did she have to be a nun?

"Please, Torrie, say something." Diana looked as if she were about to cry.

Torrie fought her desire to take Diana into her arms and comfort her. "Of course I want you to stay," she said. "I wish I could help you feel better."

"You can," Diana said. "By respecting my decision."

"Okay," Torrie said. "Not a problem. I'll do anything I can to make your stay pleasant."

"Thank you," Diana said. "You have no idea how much I appreciate it."

Torrie smiled. And you have no idea how difficult it is for me not to fight for your love, Torrie thought. It was one of the hardest things she'd ever had to do.

CHAPTER 14

Within two weeks a certified package arrived for Diana. She opened it to find her travel orders for Kenya, a one-way ticket to Nairobi, and a check for one thousand dollars to cover any unforeseen expenses, with the remainder going to the mission convent and hospital in Kenya. Diana spread the contents of the package before her on the coffee table.

A year ago, Diana thought, this would have been everything she needed to do God's will. It would have marked the beginning of a great adventure. Now it only marked the end of her time at Torrie's. She knew this day would come, but she just hadn't thought it would arrive so fast. She took a deep breath and put the papers back into the large brown envelope.

It hadn't been easy ignoring everything but friendship with Torrie. She had excused herself many evenings to go to her room to study or sleep. In fact, she got little studying done, thinking about Torrie, and sleep, when it finally came, was filled with disturbing images of Torrie. Diana felt a shiver move up her spine as she recalled bits and pieces of those dreams — holding Torrie in her arms, feeling the firm yet subtle softness of Torrie's body against her own. There were silken kisses and the imagined pleasure of being together as more than just friends.

Now, in just three weeks, she and Torrie would be separated by thousands of miles and a wide, tumultuous ocean. If only the distance could guarantee an end to her thinking and dreaming about Torrie. If only the miles could erase the sins committed in her heart. No nun was supposed to have the type of desire she felt for Torrie. She could run away from Torrie's presence, but there was nowhere to hide from herself. Not even the brick and mortar of the mother house had been able to keep Torrie from her heart. No prayer had removed the taste of Torrie's kiss from her mouth. Diana ran her fingertips lightly over her lips, remembering. *God forgive me,* she prayed. *I don't think I will ever forget her. God forgive me. I want to remember.*

* * * * *

That evening, Diana poured a second cup of coffee for herself and Torrie.

"I received my travel package today," she announced watching Torrie for her reaction.

"Travel package?" Torrie looked confused. "You didn't say anything about a vacation." She put her coffee cup on the table without taking the first swallow. "Where are you going? I thought you'd be here until your order transferred you."

"My order is transferring me." Diana felt her throat tighten and fought to keep the tears out of her eyes, her voice from cracking. "I leave for Kenya in three weeks. I'll be there for five years. If the hospital does well, I could be there ten years or longer."

Torrie's face was as pale as moonlight, and unshed tears formed a shimmery curtain over her green jade eyes. "Africa? Somehow I managed to forget that you would ever actually go." Torrie's voice seemed to come from a place deep inside her. "When do you leave?"

Diana wanted to put her arms around her, to protect her from the pain she could see in her eyes and hear in her voice. She hugged herself, trying to keep from reaching for this woman who had shaken her life to its very foundations. "I leave in three weeks."

"But there's so much more I wanted to show you. So much more . . ." Torrie's words melted into silence. Diana pressed her arms more firmly around herself. *Lord, this is much too hard,* she thought. *You'll have to help me or I will not be able to turn away from her. I mustn't offer her false hope.*

Diana cleared her throat and chose her words

carefully. "We still have time to do and see whatever you'd like. Since school is over, we can go anywhere." She forced a smile and tried to sound cheery. "We can take a vacation together. You get someone to cover for you, and we can go anywhere you'd like for a week, or even ten days." She reached out and took Torrie's hand. "You could show me the mountains you're so crazy about. Besides, we could both use the time away."

The color began to return to Torrie's face. Diana could see her consciously taking control of her emotions.

"I could get Joe Reed to cover for me. We could leave Wednesday," Torrie said.

"That sounds good to me. I've always loved the mountains." Diana felt a mixture of excitement and anxiety at the prospect of spending time alone with Torrie.

Torrie's hand closed around her own. "At least we can make your last days here memorable," Torrie said.

Diana was drawn to Torrie by some unseen magnet hidden in the dark green depths of Torrie's eyes. "All my days here have been memorable," Diana said. "No matter where I am, I'll never forget you or my time here."

CHAPTER 15

The cabin was set off by itself, surrounded by tall pines and old hickory trees. Torrie said she had purchased the cabin several years earlier. Apparently she liked the fact that the nearest neighbor was five miles away.

"This is fantastic," Diana said. "How did you find this place?" Diana set down her suitcase and began to look around the cabin.

Torrie smiled as Diana went first to the wall of windows in the large den and saw the waterfall Torrie had told her about.

"I had the chance to buy it from an old friend. It was a good opportunity." Torrie pointed at the stone fireplace at the end of the room. "It's nice at night, with a fire, and the moonlight reflecting off the waterfall."

"It sounds beautiful," Diana said. "I hate to bring up practicalities, but shouldn't we get the groceries in, and into the refrigerator?"

"You're right. I'll bring them in. The kitchen is over there." Torrie nodded toward a staircase. "The bedrooms are upstairs. Mine's to the left. Yours is at the head of the stairs. There's a full bath off each bedroom. Make yourself comfortable. I'll put the groceries up and make a pot of coffee." Torrie started for the door. "Come down when you're settled in. We'll have a cup of coffee, then I'll show you the local sights."

"It's wonderful," Diana said, looking at the painted horses and unicorns of a large carousel. "I thought these things were a thing of the past." She turned and met Torrie's bright green eyes. "How in the world did it get up the mountain to Saint Cloud? Can we ride on it? Is that allowed?" She felt like a child again. The carousel and the music reminded her of carousels she had admired in the picture books of her childhood. She waved back at three young children riding three painted horses. Hooves raised, manes flowing in the wind, mouths opened to gulp fresh air, the horses ran through imaginary meadows while the carousel carried them in never-ending circles.

"Mr. Beck owns the general store, the park and the carousel," Torrie explained. "He bought the carousel and had it shipped up here after a traveling circus went bankrupt in a town about ten miles away. It's been here ever since." She grinned. "I think the park and carousel are Mr. Beck's version of Disneyland for Saint Cloud and the neighbors." She stopped in front of Beck's General Store. "I'll be back in a minute. I'm going to get us tickets."

When the carousel stopped, Diana climbed on board and headed toward a golden palomino with a dark mane that stood in long curls whipped into place by a long-forgotten artist.

"What's your hurry?" Torrie called. "The horses aren't going anywhere."

"I already have ours picked out," Diana said. She put her foot in the palomino's stirrup and flung her leg over the painted red and brown saddle. "That one is yours." Diana pointed to a black and white pinto. "Look at those eyes. They're like burning coal."

"You certainly know your horses." Torrie smiled and reached for the leather reins. "I'd challenge you to a race, but it seems your horse is destined to lead mine by a nose, and there's nothing either of us can do to change that fact."

"No complaints, Doctor," Diana said, grinning. "Just do your best. A lesson in humility might do you a lot of good."

The music began and the carousel eased forward. Diana's horse rose as if preparing to gallop toward some finish line only carousel horses could see.

Diana looked across at Torrie, and for a moment, she could feel Torrie's body against her own, those lips brush against hers and Diana felt the heat of desire between her thighs.

Torrie was leaning toward her now, shouting something above the music. Diana blinked, refocusing her attention on the real world.

"The brass ring is coming up on your right," Torrie shouted. "Reach for the brass ring, Diana! It will bring you luck!"

If I lean a little more to my left, I could kiss her, Diana thought. She was riveted on Torrie's mouth.

"Reach for the brass ring, Diana!" Torrie shouted again.

Diana forced herself to look up. The metal arm holding the brass ring was just ahead and to her right. She leaned toward it as far as she dared, and stretched her arm out as far as it would go.

She felt her fingers close around cold metal, felt the resistance, as the carousel moved on. And then the ring snapped clear of its metal captor and slipped into her palm. She held up the prize and turned to Torrie.

"I've got it! I've got the brass ring!"

"Good for you," Torrie shouted. "If you turn it in, you'll get a free ride." Torrie looked happier than she had in weeks.

"No way!" Diana shouted. "I'm keeping this, and all the luck it can bring me."

CHAPTER 16

It was still light when Torrie and Diana sat down on a park bench to relax and enjoy the scenery.

After a while, Diana turned toward Torrie and their eyes locked, creating an emotional bridge between them. For Torrie, time stopped. She felt her heartbeat slow, heard the pulse in her ears, and held perfectly still, afraid that if she moved, the moment — the contact — would be lost forever. It was the way she felt whenever some wild creature approached her cabin in search of food. Its eyes would fix on Torrie with a look that, despite its acceptance and trust, bespoke vigilance and the ability to bolt in any direction should that trust prove ill-placed.

"Is that a real well?" Diana's words fell like a guillotine between them.

Torrie felt suddenly cold and alone. Diana nodded toward an old stone well approximately thirty yards from the bench.

"Not only is it a real well," Torrie said, "it's a wishing well."

"Really?" Diana sounded skeptical. "How many wishes has it granted you?"

"Don't tell me that someone who believes that a brass ring from a carousel can bring her luck doesn't also believe in wishing wells." Torrie was amused by Diana's childlike inconsistency. It was as if she were discovering a whole new world.

"I didn't say I don't believe in wishing wells," Diana said. "I was just curious if you'd ever cast a wish or two into it yourself." She raised an eyebrow. "Have you?"

Torrie fought a strong desire to lean forward and kiss her. She shoved her hands into her jacket pockets. "Actually, I've made quite a few. I don't remember all of them, but I do remember that the last two came true."

"What were they?" Diana asked.

Torrie laughed. "I don't remember exactly," she said. "And I'm not sure I'd tell you if I did."

"Fair enough," Diana said. "How much does it cost per wish?"

"I think my last two wishes were on nickels,"

Torrie said. She pulled two coins from her pocket and offered them to Diana. "Be my guest."

"I think I'd better wish on my own nickel," Diana said.

"I don't think it matters whose nickel gets tossed in. I doubt that the spirit in there cares one bit."

"I think you're wrong, and as a nun I know more about spirits than most people."

Torrie suddenly felt very sad. "I guess you're right. I'd almost forgotten that you're a nun."

"So had I." Diana stood up. "I know exactly what I want my first wish to be."

Torrie watched as Diana dropped a coin into its depths, then came back and sat down.

"I think that's the fastest wish I've ever seen," Torrie said.

"Fortunately, it wasn't a difficult decision," Diana said. "I'm getting hungry. Let's go back to the cabin and fix dinner."

"Not until you tell me what you wished," Torrie said.

"I'd starve to death first."

"I believe you would," Torrie said, standing. "Stubbornness is not a pretty thing in a nun. I thought all you people were supposed to be humble and obedient."

Diana grinned. "You have a lot to learn about nuns. We're as individual as physicians. Taking a vow doesn't make obedience any easier." She met Torrie's eyes. "I've always been stubborn. Vows don't change human nature. They only challenge it."

They've certainly challenged me, Torrie thought. She took a deep breath. "I guess we've both been challenged enough for one day." She looked at her watch. "Good grief! I totally forgot we're supposed to go to Mark Mason's for dinner. If we hurry we'll only be about thirty minutes late."

CHAPTER 17

A tall gray-haired man wrapped his arms around Torrie and kissed her on the cheek. "I'm so glad to see you, Torrie."

Doctor Mark Mason reminded Diana of fine, translucent china. She saw great beauty and great frailty in his lined face, pale blue eyes and thin wiry body.

He released Torrie and reached toward Diana. "And this must be Diana." His long arm curled around her shoulders. "Welcome to Saint Cloud." His pale blue eyes looked directly into hers. "Maybe we can convince you that Saint Cloud needs nurses as badly as Africa needs them."

Diana liked him immediately. "I'm sure you do, but my religious order is determined to send me to Africa to work."

"Too bad," he said. He led them into the main room of his cabin. "Make yourselves at home." He gestured toward a well worn black leather sofa and matching wing chairs that were arranged to allow the best view of the fire. He threw another log in and stoked the fire.

"Torrie, if you could help me with the pasta." He turned toward Diana. "Help yourself to the wine."

As the two old friends disappeared into the kitchen, Diana poured herself a glass of wine. An eight-by-ten photograph on a nearby bookshelf showed Torrie standing on skis in the falling snow. She was laughing and her face and eyes seemed to be lit from within.

In a single instant, Diana felt her heartbeat quicken, and she suddenly understood why women found her attractive. She drew people to herself without even trying. Diana closed her eyes. She had to stop thinking about Torrie. She'd be nothing more than another face in a long parade. No, that's not true, she chided herself. She'd be a nun who had broken her vows and made a fool of herself, all at the same time. It was a good thing she was leaving before she'd embarrassed herself and her order.

There was the sound of dishes rattling behind her, and Mark Mason's voice rolled into the room. "Dinner's finally served," he announced.

Over pasta and red clam sauce, Diana listened to Mark and Torrie discuss the clinic he had established to treat the area's sick and injured poor who couldn't afford insurance premiums, let alone the going price of a medical office visit. The clinic used a sliding scale for fees and had never turned anyone away.

When dinner was finished and the dishes cleared, the three sat with their coffee before the blazing fire.

"Are you sure you can't join us at the clinic?" Mark asked. His light blue eyes danced with the passion for what he proudly claimed was his mission in life.

"The idea is very tempting," Diana said. "But religious orders insist on running the lives of their members. My vows mean I go where my religious order tells me to go."

"Give up, Mark," Torrie said. "Diana wants to go to Africa as much as her order wants to send her there."

"No, I don't." Diana was shocked by her own words, yet amused by the surprise on Torrie's face. "It seemed like a good idea, but it would be wonderful to be able to stay right here and work in the clinic."

"I don't know much about the Catholic faith," Mark said, "but I suppose there are rules against simply quitting." There was a look of mischief in his eyes.

"I'm afraid so. The vows are binding for my lifetime."

"Most people I know find monogamy a big enough challenge," he went on, his voice sincere. "I know I've heard of nuns leaving in the past. How were they able to do that?"

"A nun can ask for a dispensation from her vows if she no longer feels called to the religious life,"

Diana explained. "It's a very serious and long, long process. In the end, the Pope has the final word."

"And what if she gets tired of waiting for him to decide and just leaves?" Mark asked. "What's he going to do? He can't have her arrested for changing her mind."

"If a nun leaves without a papal dispensation, her vows are still binding; and if she breaks those vows, she is considered to be living in sin and can no longer receive the sacraments of the Church." Diana glanced at Torrie. "As far as the Church is concerned, it's very much like a marriage. And the Church may agree to an annulment, but never to a divorce."

"In other words," he said, "you're stuck."

The words were like a physical blow. How awful, she thought. She did feel stuck at times. She shouldn't, but she did.

"If a nun feels stuck," Diana said, "she's already begun to leave."

"Speaking of leaving," Torrie said, "it's getting late and Mark has a full day tomorrow. I think we'd better be going."

Diana felt relieved. She stood up and extended her hand to him. "Thank you for a lovely evening, Mark."

"Thank you for the company." He held Diana's hand. "You're welcome here any time, dispensation or not."

"Thank you." Diana had an uneasy feeling that Mark Mason had seen deeper into her heart and mind than she cared to look herself.

CHAPTER 18

Diana knocked on Torrie's bedroom door twice with no answer. She could hear music escaping softly from inside. She turned the knob and peered into the room. The bed was turned down, but Torrie was nowhere to be seen. Two steps into the room, she noticed the opened glass sliding door and stood for a moment, admiring the view. Torrie hadn't mentioned the deck. Her eyes adjusted to the darkness and she saw Torrie, seated in the swing, her head back, staring into the night.

"Torrie," Diana spoke softly.

Torrie started. "Diana! Is anything wrong?"

"No." Diana walked onto the deck. "I thought you might like a cup of hot chocolate."

"No, thanks, but why don't you join me for a few minutes. The stars have outdone themselves tonight." Diana sat down beside Torrie and gazed upward. "It's beautiful out here. I had no idea that you had such a great view. It's fantastic!"

Torrie smiled. "It's my own personal Shangri-la. You're the first visitor to sit out here."

Flecks of starlight were reflected in Torrie's dark green eyes. God, she's beautiful, Diana thought. "I hope I'm not intruding."

"Not at all. It's nice finally to share it with someone." Torrie's face showed the hint of a smile, and she turned back toward the sky.

Diana wasn't sure she had heard Torrie correctly. "You never brought anyone special — a date — out here?"

For a moment, Torrie was silent, but the grin on Torrie's face spoke volumes. "That's right, Diana. I've never brought a date to Saint Cloud. And since you're not a date, that fact continues to be true."

Diana wondered if she looked as surprised as she felt.

Torrie laughed. "You look shocked, Diana. I think you imagine me doing a lot more dating than I do. When I have time off, I spend a lot of it up here at Mark's clinic. I'm not the party animal you might think."

Diana felt the heat rising in her cheeks and was grateful that the darkness would hide her blush. "I'm afraid what I was trying to say came out all wrong. I know you work awfully hard, and it's none of my business who you date anyway." Diana felt awkward, but she was determined not to leave Torrie with the impression that she thought badly of her. When Torrie didn't say anything, Diana went on, "I'm certainly no expert on dating. I didn't even have a date for my high school prom. It finally filtered back to me that none of the boys wanted to take a date who had already let it be known that she was entering a convent in another month. I pretended that it didn't matter. I went to the prom as a volunteer for the refreshment table. I really hoped someone would ask me to dance. Not to the fast stuff, but to music like this. Slow dancing." Diana stopped talking as the beginning notes of Chuck Mangione's "I'll Be Seeing You" floated onto the deck. "They must have played that song ten times on prom night. I really wanted someone to ask me to dance."

"Well, it's not too late," Torrie said. She stood up and extended her hand. "May I have the honor of this dance, Diana?"

Diana looked at Torrie. One dance couldn't do any harm, she thought. "I'm not a very good dancer," she said.

"Neither am I. Now give me your hand before you miss your chance again."

She took Torrie's hand and moved forward into the circle of Torrie's arms.

Diana felt her body stiffen as her cheek rested against the softness of Torrie's face.

Torrie moved her head back slightly and met Diana's eyes. "You can relax, Diana. I know you're going to Nairobi in three weeks. I won't bite. Honest."

Diana was embarrassed. "I'm sorry. I'm just not used to being in someone's arms."

"Apology accepted. Now relax and enjoy the music." She rested her cheek against Diana's and held her just a little bit closer.

Diana's heart was pounding as she relaxed her body against Torrie's. She felt fluid, complementing every curve and line of Torrie's body, merging with her completely. Suddenly they were standing still. Torrie's eyes were locked on hers, and their lips were only inches apart. Time and space had lost all meaning. Diana leaned forward and placed her lips against Torrie's. The satiny sensation sent fire into Diana's veins. For several seconds, Torrie held her close, then suddenly she relaxed her hold.

"Diana, we have to stop now," she said, her voice shaking. "This isn't what you wanted. Remember what you said about your vows."

Diana's mind was on fire, her being fused into one desire, one need — total and complete union with Torrie.

"What I said no longer matters." Diana's voice was barely a whisper. "I love you, Torrie. I think I've loved you from the first week I met you. I don't know what the future holds for us, but I do know I want to make love with you. I want you as I've never wanted anything or anyone before. I want to make love with you." Diana felt herself blushing. "I've never made love before. I don't really know how, how to touch you, how to ask you to touch me, how to please you." Torrie's silence roared in Diana's ears. "Please help me, Torrie. Please don't ask me to leave." Diana felt awkward and inadequate. "I know I'm terribly ignorant about making love. But if loving you more than I have ever loved anyone counts at all, I believe I can learn the physical part." She ran her hand along Torrie's cheek. Electric excitement ran from the tips of her fingers into every cell of her body.

Torrie clasped Diana's hand. "What you're doing is increasing my already overwhelming desire to make love to you." She brushed her lips lightly along Diana's forehead, kissed her eyes gently and held Diana's face in her hands. "As much as I want to make love to you, I don't want to cause you pain. I don't want you to do something you'll regret in the morning."

She loves me! Diana thought. *She loves me.* The thought spun in her mind like a sun about to give birth to a new world.

"The only thing I'd regret tomorrow is not making love with you tonight." Diana kissed her. "Please, Torrie, don't make me beg."

"My God, Diana, I don't want you to beg. I love you." She returned Diana's kiss. "If you change your mind at any point, tell me. It would break my heart to cause you pain."

Diana looked deeply into Torrie's green eyes. "I know what I'm saying, Torrie. I love you, and I want to make love with you." She pressed her lips against Torrie's and her mouth opened willingly as Torrie's tongue gently entered her mouth and began to explore the warmth and softness within. Torrie's tongue brushed against the inside of her upper lip, then ran against the firm softness of her tongue. Diana was filled with new and wonderful sensations that she didn't want to stop.

Diana felt a hot wetness between her thighs. She

closed her mouth around Torrie's tongue and gently sucked it deeper inside her mouth. Her body lurched forward with excitement as Torrie's hand moved between her thighs.

"Oh, God! I want you so much . . ." Diana whispered.

Torrie took her hand and led her inside to her bed.

Kissing her, Torrie untied Diana's bathrobe and pulled it from her shoulders. She slowly unbuttoned Diana's pajama top, adding new kisses as she went.

Diana was on fire with the desire to lose herself in Torrie. She shivered as Torrie caressed her breasts. Her nipples stiffened, and she longed for Torrie to take them in her mouth. The warm wetness of Torrie's tongue circled her nipples before she sucked them softly inside.

"Oh!" Diana heard the sound of her own pleasure. Her body was alive with electric energy as Torrie bent forward and kissed her mouth, as Torrie's hands found the wetness between her thighs. No more than a feathery touch, it sent pleasure racing through her body.

She lay on Torrie's bed and watched as she removed her own pajamas. Torrie's body was beautiful — the soft curve of her breasts a work of art. She reached upward and took Torrie's hand, pulling her gently down. Torrie leaned down just far enough to run her tongue over Diana's lips and push herself softly into Diana's eager mouth. Diana put her arms around Torrie's neck, kissing her deeply.

She had never felt like this before. Every cell of her body wanted Torrie completely. Every fiber of her soul wanted to merge with this woman who had touched her in places and in ways no other human being could ever have touched her before.

Diana burned with passion as Torrie lowered herself to the bed, her body a swatch of silk against Diana's skin.

Torrie's body covered her completely. Diana held her tighter and turned in search of Torrie's mouth as she felt burning kisses sear her neck, shoulders and breasts. Torrie was everywhere at once, gliding downward, downward toward the ache between Diana's thighs.

"Torrie, wait." Diana's heart was racing. She could hardly breathe. She felt faint with pleasure as Torrie's fingers grazed the wet silk between her legs. Diana's words came in short breathless gasps as she pulled Torrie toward her. "Are you sure you want to do this?" Torrie's green eyes were like molten jade.

"I'm very sure, Diana." Torrie kissed her passionately. "I love you, Diana." Torrie started to kiss her way downward again.

Again, Diana pulled her upward. "I'm afraid you'll be disappointed."

Torrie kissed Diana's forehead. Her fingers never stopped moving between Diana's thighs. "That feels wonderful," Diana said. "But I want to make you feel wonderful too."

"I already do," Torrie said.

"I want to make love to you." Diana held Torrie's face between her hands and kissed her, exploring the ridges of the roof of her mouth. She looked into Torrie's eyes again. "I love you. I don't want to disappoint you."

"You couldn't disappoint me," Torrie said. "You

can make love to me later. And believe me, there is nothing you could do that I wouldn't like, that wouldn't bring me pleasure." She kissed Diana again, and again began her journey downward.

Torrie's kisses flamed against Diana's inner thighs. They entered her and swam through her veins, filling her with the heat of passion. Diana's legs parted willingly and she pushed her hips downward, seeking more contact.

She sighed loudly as she felt the first touch of Torrie's tongue brush against her and separate the silken folds.

Diana ran her hands through Torrie's hair and guided her closer to the fire growing between her thighs. Diana's joy increased as Torrie's mouth closed around her, gently sucking the pearl into her mouth. Her strokes were light at first, and as they grew in intensity, Diana's pleasure rose to a crescendo. With one final spark, Diana felt herself exploding into a thousand fiery comets, scattered through a universe of their making. She could feel Torrie in each discrete part of herself.

Suddenly she was holding Torrie tightly against herself. Torrie's body covered her like a second skin. Torrie was kissing her, running her tongue lightly over Diana's lips, against her eyelashes, against the nape of her neck.

"I love you, Diana," Torrie whispered. "I love you."

Diana looked at Torrie and brushed her fingertips over Torrie's mouth. "I love you." Diana felt tears in her eyes. "I love you more than I have ever loved anything or anybody." Then she remembered. "I don't know how I can ever give you up."

Torrie kissed her softly. "Don't think about that now. Just think about us. I know we were meant to be together. I won't give you up that easily, Diana."

Diana felt safe and secure. Drowsiness began to overtake her. "I love you, Torrie." She closed her eyes. "I'm falling to sleep and I want to make love to you."

She felt Torrie's fingers trailing over her face and neck.

"Let yourself sleep, Diana. I'll be right here. We'll make love in the morning."

Diana nestled her head against Torrie's shoulder.

In seconds she was asleep, dreaming of Torrie.

CHAPTER 19

So this was what it's like to wake up with the person you love, Diana thought. Perhaps that was why so many people equated "making love" and "sleeping together."

The sound of Torrie's rhythmic breathing filled the room. She watched the rise and fall of her chest and traced the outline of her breast. The nipples became firm, and Diana felt a tightness below. She shivered as she remembered the total pleasure Torrie had given her. Not even God had compelled her like this; not even God had made her feel so loved, so accepted. Not even God had filled the vacant lonely places in her heart. Now she knew what it meant to be "us" instead of "me," "we" instead of "I." She ran her hand lightly over Torrie's cheek. God couldn't have brought them together without knowing what the result would be. He couldn't expect her to give Torrie up. They were in love, and now she knew what loving and being loved meant.

Diana's fingertips moved slowly, deliberately, in smaller and smaller circles, until she felt Torrie's nipple stiffen again. Even in sleep her body responded. Diana was amazed. She kissed Torrie's lips. They tasted salty and sweet.

"I want to make love to you," Diana whispered.

Torrie moved slowly, stretching out, opening herself, making herself vulnerable. Hesitantly, Diana placed her hand on the silken skin of Torrie's inner thigh. She shuddered with excitement, and a little bit of fear, as her fingers touched the satin folds between Torrie's thighs. What if she disappointed her? Torrie moved again, pressing downward against her.

"Torrie," Diana said quietly. "Torrie."

Torrie's eyes fluttered, and she smiled at Diana. She pulled Diana close and kissed her, gently at first, the passion and intensity increasing. Her tongue felt hot and insistent.

"I want you to make love to me, Diana. I want you more than I've ever wanted anyone."

Diana traced Torrie's nipples with her tongue, held them gently between her teeth, and sucked them into her mouth. Passion rose inside her, racing through her body.

"That feels wonderful." Torrie gasped. "Don't stop."

Diana had no intention of stopping. She could still feel Torrie's touch against and inside her, small fires connected by smoldering memories. Diana followed the light from the fires Torrie had ignited in her body. She moved with slow deliberation.

Her fingers glided into the wet, hot furnace and stroked the soft inner walls.

"Move your fingers upward, Diana," Torrie whispered breathlessly.

Diana obeyed immediately and was delighted as she heard Torrie gasp, and felt her body shudder with pleasure. Diana kissed her way downward, along Torrie's narrow waist and flat stomach, along the tight muscles and taut skin of Torrie's abdomen, to the smooth skin of Torrie's inner thighs.

Diana felt her own stomach tighten as Torrie threaded her fingers through her hair and, with a slight pressure, guided her head upward so that her mouth met the swollen lips. Diana's tongue glided to the pure, silky pearl of pleasure which grew firm under the strokes, and swelled as Diana sucked it inside her mouth. Its pulse beat against her tongue, and she pushed her fingers inside, exploring the upper walls.

"Faster, Diana." Torrie's voice was hoarse.

Diana complied, sucking and stroking faster and harder, moving her head from side to side, holding the firmness in her teeth and moving her fingers fast and hard deep inside Torrie. She felt herself dissolving into the white heat of their passion, felt herself merging with Torrie.

"Harder," Torrie cried. "Harder!"

Diana pushed her tongue harder against Torrie and doubled her strokes. She felt dizzy with happiness as she felt Torrie grow larger and firmer inside her mouth, felt the soft walls inside Torrie close tighter against her fingers.

"Diana," Torrie called. "Oh, Diana!"

Torrie's muscles contracted and let go. Diana tasted the warm salty liquid covering her fingers, hand and wrist. Torrie's muscles clamped her fingers tightly; her body arched and began to shudder. Torrie's hands pushed deeper into Diana's hair and pressed Diana's head firmly against herself. Diana's own pleasure rose like a gathering storm. And then, Torrie screamed and she knew Torrie was enveloped in total pleasure. The knowledge and excitement pushed Diana past the point of ordinary pleasure, into a world where she and Torrie were locked in a dance of exquisite and ultimate rapture. Diana closed her eyes and saw streams of vibrant color, scarlet and purple. Rapture, she thought, this was rapture.

Suddenly she was being pulled upward. Torrie's arms closed around her and she covered Diana with hungry, joyful kisses. Diana felt merged with Torrie in body and spirit.

"I love you, Diana," Torrie whispered in a hoarse voice. "I've never felt so close to anyone before, so complete."

Diana felt happy, proud and fulfilled. She kissed Torrie's eyes, her nose, her mouth. "I'm so glad you're pleased." She rested her head on Torrie's shoulder. She wanted to study her body. She wanted to know every curve, every hollow, every special place where she liked to be touched or kissed, every place where she'd never been kissed before....She kissed her passionately on the mouth.

"I love you, Torrie. I love you more than myself. I love you more than God."

CHAPTER 20

The next morning they slept late, then spent the afternoon taking a long walk. That evening Diana prepared her family's favorite pizza while Torrie built a fire. Finally, everything was ready and Diana waited expectantly as Torrie took a bite.

"Well?" Diana said. "Is it or isn't it the best pizza you've ever tasted?"

Torrie nodded and took another bite.

The light from the fireplace danced along Torrie's body as the flames climbed into the air and retreated, only to begin their climb again. In her mind, Diana replayed scenes from their lovemaking, and for a moment, she completely forgot her own question. The memory of Torrie's body, the touch of her skin, the curves of her breasts, the taste of her kiss, banished all other thoughts. In a little less than a week, she had grown so close to Torrie that it was as if the two had been journeying toward each other since they were children. Older memories played through her mind — memories of vows, her promises to a God she had taken as her lover, memories of a lover who had never elicited the feelings in her that Torrie had called forth.

Torrie's voice sliced through her thoughts.

"It's very, very good."

"What?" Diana said. She fought to refocus her attention.

Torrie laughed. "Your pizza." She held up her plate. "I agree it's the best I ever tasted. But you don't look as if you're thinking about pizza." Torrie put her plate down and took Diana's hand. "Where are you?"

"Right here." Diana squeezed Torrie's hand. "It's just really hit me that this is our last night here. I'm not looking forward to going back to Atlanta tomorrow. It scares me."

Tiny flames reflected in Torrie's eyes, beautiful green fire. Diana wanted to feel Torrie's arms around her again.

"I don't want to lose you." Diana felt the tightness of tears in her throat.

Torrie brushed tears from Diana's cheeks.

"You're not going to lose me." Torrie kissed the back of Diana's hand. "I love you, Diana. I want you with me as long as you choose to stay."

"That will mean the rest of our lives," Diana said.

"That's exactly what I had in mind." Torrie leaned forward and kissed her. "Forever."

"I'm not sure you realize the problems that will confront us when my order and my parents find out I'm leaving the convent." Diana studied Torrie's face, hoping to glean the answer she wanted. "It could get pretty rocky."

"Diana, if I could marry you legally, I would. I can't imagine my life without you." Torrie kissed Diana's eyes and brushed more tears from her cheeks. "No matter what it takes, no matter what it costs, no matter what we have to go through, I want you to share my life with me. Whatever problems come up, we'll solve. Together."

Diana wiped her tears away and smiled at Torrie. Love and desire welled up inside her like an ocean tide caught in the pull of a full moon. *Lord, I love this woman,* she thought.

Diana leaned forward and ran her fingertips along Torrie's lips. She pressed her mouth against Torrie's and slowly slipped her tongue inside. Passion flowed through her, churning between her thighs. She slipped her hand beneath Torrie's sweater, to the warmth of her skin.

"I want you," Diana whispered against Torrie's lips as she pushed her tongue deeper.

Torrie's hands were all over her, moving along her body like a hot summer breeze, leaving a flame-scorched path in their wake.

Diana yielded to the weight of Torrie's body pressed against her. She lay on her back on the soft, black alpaca rug in front of the fireplace.

The fire crackled and popped, blending with the music of Kenny G. The wall of cathedral windows seemed to lift everything in the room upward. Diana's passion mounted as Torrie removed her clothing, kissing the places it had covered.

Diana's body sank into the softness of the alpaca rug, and the heat from the fire felt warm and assuring against her naked skin. She reached up, removed Torrie's sweater and let it fall next to her own discarded clothing.

"You have a beautiful body," Diana said. "I love undressing you. It's like opening Christmas presents." She ran her fingers over Torrie's nipples. "And getting exactly what I wanted."

Diana closed her eyes as Torrie pulled off the rest of her clothing and stretched out on top of her. Diana's pleasure deepened as Torrie kissed her lips, her lashes, the curve of her ear. With soft lips, she kissed her way down Diana's neck and shoulders, then returned to her mouth.

Diana caressed Torrie's breasts, squeezing the nipples gently between her fingers.

In one graceful movement, Torrie wrapped her arms around Diana and rolled over, holding Diana close. "I want to taste you. Kneel over me, Diana. I want to make love to you and feel you inside my mouth."

Torrie's words struck new fires inside Diana. She took a pillow from the sofa, placed it beneath Torrie's head, and leaned down and kissed her. "I love you, Torrie." Firelight and moonlight were green in the pools of Torrie's eyes.

She knelt over Torrie and slowly lowered herself

to within inches of Torrie's mouth. Her heart skipped a beat as Torrie cradled her hips and guided her gently downward.

With feather strokes, Torrie began. Passion's fire burned through Diana's body and inflamed her soul. She wove her fingers through Torrie's soft curls and arched her back. Enfolded in the firm strokes of Torrie's tongue, she rode Torrie's rhythms from one pleasure to another. Boundaries lost, her head spun, and she shuddered with ecstasy. She held tightly to Torrie's head, as the firmness of Torrie's mouth produced wave after wave of orgasmic pleasure. Neither of them, Diana thought, would ever be quite the same again.

Exhausted, Diana fell to the warm rug. She pressed her mouth against Torrie's and tasted the love that had formed new bonds between them. Her lips glided in the sweet, salty wetness they had created.

"I love you, Torrie." Diana spoke without taking her mouth from Torrie's. "I want to make love to you."

"You just did, my darling." Torrie kissed Diana's eyes, forehead and lips. "I am as completely satisfied as you."

Diana nestled closer and she realized that Torrie had covered them with the eiderdown comforter from the sofa.

"Are you warm enough?" Torrie asked.

"I'm perfect," Diana said without opening her eyes. "We're perfect."

Torrie kissed her forehead. "I couldn't agree more."

Diana wrapped her arms around Torrie and drifted into sleep, and dreams of their future.

CHAPTER 21

Like a diver rising too quickly from a great depth to the surface, Torrie opened her eyes and squinted at the bright sunlight. For a moment no solid thoughts formed in her mind. It was as if she were drunk from too much nitrogen in her blood. She sat up quickly and propped herself against a pillow.

She scanned the floor by the fireplace, looking for their clothes. They were gone. She shook herself awake, then heard the faint sounds of someone moving about the kitchen. A few seconds later Diana came into the room, carrying a breakfast tray. She looked happy and warm, wrapped in her white terrycloth bathrobe.

"Good morning." She set the tray on Torrie's lap. "I thought you might like some coffee and an English muffin." She leaned over and kissed her lightly on the lips. Torrie put her arm around Diana and kissed her more deeply.

"I was afraid I'd dreamed what happened last night," Torrie said. "I'm glad I didn't."

Diana smiled and her dark brown eyes grew brighter. "It was no dream. I remember every wonderful detail." She poured two cups of coffee and spread jam on an English muffin.

Torrie's mind was crowded with thoughts and she felt slightly uncomfortable. Diana seemed fine. Better than fine. She seemed happy. There was no sign of remorse on her face or in her eyes.

She reached out, took Diana's hand in her own, and asked the question she most feared. "Any regrets about this week?"

"One or two," Diana said. She kissed the back of Torrie's hand and looked directly into her eyes.

Torrie's heart plummeted. The mere suggestion that she might have caused Diana pain was enough to make her wish that nothing had happened between them.

"I was afraid this might happen." Torrie felt sick to her stomach. "All I can do is apologize." She watched Diana closely. "I love you, and I don't know what I'll do without you. If I had my way, we'd make a commitment to each other and live the rest of our lives together. But I don't want you to live a life you'd regret each day."

Diana held Torrie's face between her hands.

"Torrie, my only regrets are that I fought so long against my feelings, and that I didn't tell you sooner that I'm in love with you."

Torrie felt as if a terrible weight had been lifted from her heart. "You do want a life with me? This week hasn't been a dream? That *is* what you're saying, isn't it?"

Diana laughed. "You bet I want a life with you! I want us to grow old together. To sit on your deck and discuss the best ways to deal with arthritis. The best ways to cope with my parents and brother, who will never accept our relationship."

"You'd give up the convent not to mention the Church . . . and your family's approval in order to share a life with me?" Torrie could feel the tears running down her cheeks.

"I already have. I love you, Torrie. I couldn't turn back now, no matter what happens."

Torrie set the breakfast tray aside and took Diana into her arms. "I know we'll be happy together. Whatever problems come up, we'll work through them." Torrie kissed her passionately. "I want to make love to you again," Torrie whispered into her ear.

"If you're looking for an argument, you won't get one from me."

Both women jumped when the telephone rang. It hadn't rung all week.

"Do you have to answer it?" Diana asked.

"I'm afraid so," Torrie said. "It could be about a patient."

Torrie lifted the receiver. "Hello, this is Doctor Lassiter." She listened, then responded, "Sure, Mark. What time do you want to see me today?" Torrie looked surprised. She glanced at Diana and shrugged. "Okay, I'll be there." She replaced the receiver. "I'm sorry, Diana. Mark wants to see me." She felt caught. "I couldn't say no."

"Of course not," Diana said. "I'll take a rain check." She kissed Torrie. "I'll go take a shower."

"You can take one with me," Torrie said.

"Not right now," Diana grinned. "We'd never get out of here, let alone stop at Mark's."

Torrie laughed. "Right! I'll see you in a few minutes. Dressed."

"Are you sure you don't want to come in?" Torrie asked. She looked at Diana and felt a strong desire to kiss her.

"I'll wait in the car. I need to think about how I'm going to break the news to my family. Tell Mark I said hello."

"I will. I won't be long."

Torrie climbed the steps and knocked on the door. Mark Mason opened the door immediately. He looked unusually serious.

"What's wrong, Mark? You look as if you just lost your best friend." She followed Mark to the fireplace and sat down in the worn black leather chair across from him.

Mark was looking directly at her, but for several minutes, he said nothing.

Torrie waited. This wasn't like him, she thought. He usually spoke his mind without hesitation.

"Torrie, I have something to tell you." Mark's tone was solemn and there were tears in his eyes. "Russ Kirkland called me last night."

"Kirkland?" Torrie was surprised. "Are you ill,

Mark?" Torrie leaned forward. "You never said anything to me. How can I help?"

Mark Mason's face was wet with tears. "He called me about you. They finally completed all the tests, including the second set, concerning your headaches. He feels certain that they've pinpointed the cause."

Torrie felt suddenly cold and afraid. "I was probably being overcautious to go to Kirkland to begin with. I've never felt better in my life. I feel wonderful." She was very defensive, she knew, but couldn't stop herself. "I am as healthy as a proverbial horse."

Mark glanced upward for a moment, then looked directly at her. "No, Torrie, you're not. Russ Kirkland had the Chief of Neurology at Johns Hopkins evaluate your history and test results. She in turn had two of her associates do the same. I spoke with all three of them by conference call late last night. After a thirty minute discussion, I have to accept that the diagnosis they reached is correct." Mark took a deep breath and exhaled slowly. "You have a rare brain tumor."

The words hit Torrie like a physical blow. Brain tumor? Her headaches weren't severe enough to support that diagnosis. There had to be some mistake. She pushed herself to ask questions, not at all certain that she wanted to hear the answers.

"What do they advise?" Torrie asked. "Surgery? Radiation? A combination?"

"It's too late for them, Torrie."

"Too late!" Torrie was devastated. "There must be some mistake. I have no symptoms. My headaches aren't that bad."

"According to Bloom, you won't experience

excruciating pain. She's only seen two other cases like it in her twenty-five years of practice."

"No radiation or surgery," Torrie felt sick to her stomach. This couldn't really be happening.

"I explored all possible therapies with Bloom and her two associates. All three agree that you're not a candidate for surgery or radiation."

Torrie felt stunned. "No treatment? What are they talking about? Are you telling me that I'm dying?"

"We're all dying," Mark said. "Some of us just know a little more about when and how."

"Don't play games with me." Torrie was annoyed and angry. "Am I dying? How long do I have? A month? A year? A week?" She wanted to hear the truth.

"About nine months. Maybe a year." Mark's voice was barely above a whisper, his face was pale.

"And the end?" Torrie steeled herself for the answer. "Tell me."

"You'll have a headache, but no more severe than those you've had in the past. You'll know it's different because your vision will start to fade. It will fade gradually over a very short period of time. At the end of that time, you'll be blind. Ten to fifteen minutes later, you'll lose consciousness. Death will come five or ten minutes later while you're in a coma." Rivers of silent tears made their way down Mark's face.

How neat and tidy it all sounds, Torrie thought.

"I wish there were something I could do or say to make it all better," Mark said. "I've never felt more powerless as a physician."

"Neither have I. It's as if the gods waited for the worst possible moment to put this in my life. A year

111

ago, I might not have cared so much." Torrie stood up and began to pace. "Today I care. I care a great deal. I want to live to be at least one hundred and fifty." She looked at Mark and recognized the love in her friend's eyes.

Poor Mark, she thought. She rested her hand on his shoulder.

"I know how hard it must have been for you to tell me, how hard it must be to want to help and know there's nothing medicine can do." She started to pace again. "I don't want to die now, Mark. Not now when life has just become so precious to me." She stopped and looked at him. "For the first time in my life, I'm in love. *Really* in love. I have a relationship that will grow deeper and richer with each passing day. A relationship that I want to nourish and grow in, a love that means more to me than medicine, or money, or my life."

Mark's pale blue eyes were filled with understanding and pain. "It's Diana, isn't it? You're in love with her."

Torrie felt as if her heart were already broken. "Yes. We're very much in love." She sat back down. "And now I'll have to send her away without letting her know why." Torrie closed her eyes and squeezed them tight in an effort to stop her own tears. "How can I send her away? What will I do without her?"

CHAPTER 22

Torrie had been unusually silent during the trip back to Atlanta. When they arrived, she helped unpack the car and excused herself to make a phone call.

Diana was on her second cup of coffee when Torrie finally came into the den and sat down next to her.

"Is everything all right?" Diana was concerned. "You're awfully pale."

Torrie's face seemed strangely inexpressive, and

the energy that usually enlivened her green eyes, seemed nowhere in sight.

"Diana, I'm not quite sure how to tell you what I'm about to say, and I'm pretty sure there's no way to make it sound any better."

Diana felt the uneasiness that so often precedes a storm. The world had somehow tilted suddenly and nothing seemed exactly as it had before they left Saint Cloud. She looked at Torrie and waited.

"Whatever it is," Diana said finally. "We can work it out together."

"No, we can't." The uncaring, stern tone frightened Diana and led her to expect a more powerful blow. Torrie's face was devoid of emotion. "I've made a horrible mistake, Diana," Torrie continued in an almost monotone voice. "I allowed myself to be carried away by the moment and the surroundings."

Diana felt as if someone were playing a horrible joke on her. This wasn't Torrie at all. Not the Torrie she had made love with.

Torrie's eyes were no longer focused on her. "I should never have made love with you," she said.

The words cut into Diana like a scalpel. *Should never have made love with me,* she repeated silently.

"It's been a long time since I allowed myself to be flattered by someone's obvious infatuation for me." Torrie glanced at her then went on. "I don't think you should leave the convent on account of me. It would only compound the damage already done. You need to go to Africa just as you had planned."

Diana was suddenly nauseous. Could these words actually be coming from Torrie? What could have changed in so brief a time? Diana had already committed herself spiritually, physically and emotionally to Torrie. Torrie had returned her love, had made plans with her. The commitment was mutual.

"I don't understand," Diana began. She heard her words as if they were spoken by someone else. "If I go to Africa . . ." She couldn't complete her sentence. Her legs were trembling, and she needed to sit down.

"No one knows what happened between us," Torrie said. "You can report to Nairobi just as planned. It will give us time to think this through."

"I don't need time to think things through." Diana felt on the verge of panic. Lightheadedness increased her nausea; she wondered if she would have to excuse herself. She took a deep breath. "I love you. I don't want to go to Africa. I want to be with you."

"I need time to think," Torrie said. "I'm not sure I want a commitment right now. I know this must sound terrible after our time at Saint Cloud, but a second bad decision won't make my first mistake any less hurtful."

"What are you saying?" Diana was swimming through a flood of contradictory feelings. Confusion and anger gripped her. "Are you saying that you don't love me? That you made love with me by mistake?"

"I'm very attracted to you, Diana, but I'm not sure I love you. It wouldn't be right to let you leave the convent for me when I'm not sure exactly what I feel for you."

"I can't believe you're telling me this!" Diana felt helpless. "You told me you loved me less than three hours ago. What changed your mind?"

"I'm not sure," Torrie said. "Does it really matter?"

Anger consumed her. "Yes, it really matters to me what changed your mind. I want to know the truth. That's not asking a lot, Torrie. I'm not asking to stay here tonight. You're not my prisoner or my trophy. You have the right to change your mind. But I have to know why."

Torrie was staring at her. There was a tiny flicker of energy visible in her eyes. "I told you, I don't know. Do you want me to just make something up?" Torrie's tone had a sharp edge.

"I don't believe you!" Diana shouted. "You're lying to me. I want the truth."

Torrie's eyes snapped with anger. "I don't owe you a thing. Now get your things and get out of here." Torrie stood up and began to pace. "You should be able to be packed by morning. I'll drive you to the airport or anywhere else you like." She stopped and stared down at Diana. "But I want you out of my house."

"And I still want to know why!" Diana yelled. She was determined not to leave without an explanation.

The sound of the phone cut between them like a referee.

"I'll get it," Diana said. She started toward the phone.

"Let it ring!" Torrie shouted.

"It might be someone from the mother house. If you want me out of here, I should answer it," Diana said.

"I'll get it," Torrie said. She shoved past Diana and answered in a calm voice. "Yes, we made it back fine . . . I can't really talk now, Mark. Can I call you back in about an hour? . . . Yes. I'll give it serious consideration." She replaced the receiver and faced Diana. "I really don't want to fight with you. Please respect my wishes." Torrie's face was no longer a mask. It reflected a mixture of love and fear.

"What does Mark want you to consider seriously?" Diana suspected that Mark's call was connected to Torrie's odd behavior.

"Something about a patient," Torrie said. "Now, I'd like you to get your things together."

"I'd like the truth." Diana moved to within inches of Torrie. "Whatever it is."

Torrie bit her lower lip and looked away.

"Does your change of mind have something to do with Mark Mason's patient?" Diana reached out and lifted Torrie's chin upward so she could see her eyes. They were filled with tears. With a sinking feeling, she watched Torrie closely. Her skin was pasty. "It's you, isn't it?" Diana fought to form her thoughts into words. "Something's wrong."

Tears were streaming down Torrie's face. She was shaking with the force of her sobs as she choked out the words. "I'm dying." Her eyes were veiled in tears, as she told Diana the diagnosis, and even her lips had lost their color.

"My God, Torrie, were you really going to send me away without telling me?" She wrapped her arms around Torrie and held her tightly. Torrie's tears felt hot against the coldness of her skin. Diana tightened the circle of her arms, desperate to shelter Torrie inside herself. "Don't you know that you're my home now? Where would I go without you?"

Diana brushed her cheek lightly against Torrie's,

mixing their tears, making them theirs, absorbing her pain, making it shared.

"I love you, Torrie," she whispered into Torrie's ear. "I love you more than I ever thought possible. Whatever happens, we'll face it together."

"I love you, Diana," Torrie said through her sobs. "I'm so glad you don't want to leave."

"Then you and I are finished with the subject of my leaving," Diana said, kissing her.

"Yes," Torrie said. "I'll never mention it again."

"Good," Diana said. "Now we can get on with the rest of our lives together."

CHAPTER 23

Diana's hands felt soft and smooth as she stroked Torrie's forehead. Torrie's emotions were a mixture of sadness, love and dread. She felt protected as she lay on the sofa, her head nestled in Diana's lap.

She watched the bright tapering flames consuming the oak and hickory wood Diana had stacked in the fireplace. Slender fingers of fire stretched upward, as if searching for something beyond their reach, and as if in protest, the burning logs popped and hissed, sending showers of sparks beyond the fire screen and into the room. They hung suspended, hovering like fireflies until they gave their brightest light and disappeared forever.

"The fire is beautiful," Torrie said. The flames had a soothing effect on her.

"You're beautiful," Diana said. Her voice was calm and comforting. She ran her fingertips along Torrie's cheek.

Torrie looked up into Diana's velvet brown eyes. "I feel beautiful when you look at me like that," Torrie said. She felt loved and desired. Their kiss was warm and tender.

Diana sat back and met Torrie's eyes. "Weren't you going to call Mark back?"

Torrie looked at her watch. "Yes. It's getting late. I'd better call him now." She sat up. "I wish I knew what to say to him. I know how bad he feels. Physicians don't like being powerless."

"Tell him you want another opinion," Diana said.

Torrie felt sadness wash over her. She clasped Diana's hands between her own and searched her eyes for understanding. "Another opinion won't change anything. Kirkland referred me to Janice Bloom because she's one of the top neurosurgeons in the country." She shook her head. "I didn't believe there was anything seriously wrong with me. It's funny, I never even called for the test results. If Mark hadn't talked with me, I still wouldn't know the truth." She forced a smile. "It seems I'm a better ostrich than I ever dreamed."

"Won't you at least get another opinion concerning possible treatments?" Diana's eyes spoke the plea that didn't sound in her voice.

"If it would do any good, I'd see a hundred specialists." Torrie wanted Diana to understand. "But

120

I don't want my life extended for even an hour if that hour holds only pain and endurance for both of us. I want us to have a *good* life together, no matter what its length."

"But we can't just give up. I don't want to lose you, and I won't give you up one minute before it's inevitable." Diana's voice was filled with determination.

"How very lucky I am to have you love me," Torrie said. She wrapped Diana in her arms and kissed her passionately on the mouth. "I'll see anyone who Mark and Bloom agree on — for one month. After that, if there's no improvement in the prognosis, you and I must get on with living our lives together." Torrie kissed her. "I want you to agree with that, Diana. I want your promise."

"But what if —"

Torrie rested her fingers against Diana's lips. "I want your word, Diana. That way we'll have time for more important things."

"I promise," Diana said.

"Good," Torrie said. "I'll call Mark in the morning."

"Thank you," Diana said.

"You may not thank me when your order and family disown you." Torrie knew she was speaking her fear and hoping for reassurance.

"You're my family now," Diana said. "Nothing else matters. If it's all right with you, I intend to tell my order and my family exactly why I'm leaving. I don't want to waste one minute fabricating lies to hide the fact that I'm in love with a wonderful woman and intend to spend my life with her."

A log shifted on the fire and shot out bright new flames that threw a warm golden light over Diana.

"Are you sure you want to do that, Diana?" Torrie was concerned. "You have no idea how vicious people can be ... how they can disown you completely."

Diana shrugged her shoulders. "If that's how it has to be, I'll be sorry, but I will not spend one second wasting our time on lies." Diana sounded adamant. "I'm proud of the fact that we love each other. I won't diminish that love by degrading it with lies."

Torrie was surprised and delighted at Diana's staunch stance. "I'm proud of you, Diana." Torrie squeezed her hand.

Diana yawned and covered her mouth. "I'm sorry, I guess I'm more tired than I realized."

"Me too," Torrie said. "Let's go to bed. We can call Mark in the morning after a good night's sleep."

Within a week, Diana and Torrie were headed for different cities: Torrie to Baltimore and Johns Hopkins for further neurological testing; and Diana for Buffalo, her parents, and the mother house of the Sisters of the Holy Spirit. She would inform both, that she was leaving the convent to make a life with the woman she loved.

CHAPTER 24

It was nearly noon when Diana caught a taxi at the Buffalo Airport and took the thirty-minute ride to her parents' home. She paid the driver and walked slowly up the driveway.

Diana hesitated a moment before she rang the doorbell at the side door to her parent's house. This was not going to be easy, she thought as she took a deep breath and pressed the bell. Suddenly her knees were shaking, and tiny beads of sweat covered her forehead, despite the cool autumn air of Buffalo.

Diana felt her heartbeat quicken as the door

opened and her mother stood before her in obvious shock.

"Diana!" her mother exclaimed. "I thought you were on your way to Africa!" She reached out and hugged her daughter. "Come in, come in! I was just making lunch. Your father is fixing the washing machine for the second time this month. This retirement is driving me crazy. All he tries to do is fix things. The clothes are still sopping wet when I go to put them in the dryer." She walked to the basement door and called, "Joe, Diana's here! Come on up and visit with your daughter." She turned and studied Diana. "You look pale." She put her hand on Diana's forehead. "Are you sick? Is that why you're not on your way to Africa?"

Diana felt queasy. She took her mother's hand. "I'm not sick, Mom. I just need to talk to you and Dad. I won't be going to Africa."

The basement door slammed shut and her father lumbered into the room. "What's that?" he asked in a loud voice. "Not going to Africa? Why not? Are you sick?" He turned to his wife. "She looks sick. Look how pale she is. I don't have a shirt that white." He went into the living room and sat down in his favorite overstuffed chair.

"She says she's not sick, Joe." Her mother placed a plate of sandwiches on the coffee table and joined Diana on the sofa.

"Yeah? Well, that's good." Her father selected a sandwich. "But how come you're not on your way to Africa? Did they give your job to someone else?"

"No, but they will," Diana said. "I'm going by the mother house when I leave. When I tell them what

I'm about to tell you, I'm sure someone else will be sent in my place."

"Diana, this was a plum assignment." Her father was clearly disappointed. "What could you possibly have done to lose this job? Nuns don't lose assignments. I never heard of such a thing." He turned toward his wife. "Have you?"

"No, Joe, I haven't. The Sisters always seemed like saints to me."

Diana felt sick to her stomach. Don't panic, she told herself. Just stick to the plan and tell them the truth. It would be a lot easier, Diana thought, if the decision to tell them affected only her. But it didn't. It would change the way her parents saw themselves, and it would change the way their neighbors and friends saw them. They weren't going to like it, but they did need to hear it.

Diana took a deep breath. "Mom, Dad." She felt as if she were stepping off the Empire State Building. "I didn't lose my assignment to Africa. I've made a decision that means I'll have to give it up." Her parents looked as if they had been slapped in the face. "God, I wish there were a painless way to do this. There isn't." She leaned forward. "I've decided to leave the convent. I'm going to tell Reverend Mother."

"I don't believe what I'm hearing!" Diana's mother looked thoroughly confused. "You wanted to be a nun since you were a little girl. Why would you change your mind after all this time?"

"I don't understand either," her father said. "You've got a nice clean life. You don't have to worry where your next meal is coming from; or how you're going to pay the rent; or whether or not your husband is seeing another woman. You've got it pretty good compared to most women. Why in God's name would you want to leave?"

Diana looked from her father to her mother, and said to her father, "Because for the first time in my life, I'm in love, and I want to share my life with my lover."

"Your lover!" His face was dark red. "You're a nun! Nuns don't have . . . lovers. What happened to your vow of chastity? He's dishonored himself by seducing a nun, and you, too. Treating you as if you were just any woman." He stood up and began to pace. "You're not pregnant, are you?" He stopped and looked at her.

"No, I'm not pregnant," she said.

"That's a relief. This can still be handled by damage control." More involved in what he was saying than in hearing Diana out, he went on. "I need to talk to this guy to let him know the harm he's causing. Is he in Buffalo with you?"

Her mother was silent.

Diana wanted the conversation to be over. Why couldn't it just be simple? She met her father's eyes directly. "I came to Buffalo by myself."

"What kind of man would let you come up here alone?" Her father's voice was filled with contempt.

"It's not a man, Dad." Diana exerted great control to keep her voice calm and conversational. "She's not with me because she's very ill. She's in the hospital for tests. I'm in love with her. We're hoping —"

Diana's mother gasped and covered her mouth.

"You're what!" Her father shouted. "Her? You're in love with a woman? If this is a joke, Diana, it isn't funny! And if it isn't a joke, it's a tragedy!"

"It's neither," Diana said. "It's simply the truth. We plan to live the rest of our lives together." If only her parents would realize that her love for Torrie was a good thing, a beautiful thing. "I think you'll feel differently about the whole thing after you meet her. She's sensitive, bright, committed to helping others. She's a very talented physician."

"Stop it, Diana!" her father shouted. "I won't have you talking about this abomination as if it were something to be proud of. I won't have you tell me this pervert is wonderful and good! This pervert seduced my daughter, seduced a bride of Christ! She's sick. God is punishing her for her evil."

"That's an awful thing to say!" Diana felt the anger rising inside her. "God doesn't do things like that, and Torrie is anything but evil."

"She's a pervert, Diana. A queer! Look what you did to your mother." He put his hand on his wife's shoulder. She was sobbing quietly, tears streaming down her face.

Diana felt terrible about causing her mother pain. "I'm so sorry you're hurt, Mom. I would never hurt you intentionally."

"Of course you wouldn't." Her father's voice was eerily calm and quiet. "You've always been a joy to us. It's obvious that you've been seduced. You'll go to Meyer Memorial to get help so you can get away from her. The order need never know about any of it. Your mother and I will pay for your psychiatric care. That way you'll remain in the convent and eventually be able to go to Africa just as you'd planned."

"Dad, I'm not crazy. I'm in love. I don't need psychiatric help. I don't even need your support, although I'd like to have it, along with your blessing."

"It hurts me to have tell you this, Diana, but there's no way we could endorse this sort of perversion. You've made a terrible mistake. Let us help you undo your mistake."

"Dad, I love this woman. I'm not about to give her up. I'd like you to understand, but if you can't or won't, we'll get by."

"Then you'll get by," her father said. "But if you persist in this perversion, we'll be forced to disown you."

Her mother said nothing.

Diana felt as if a knife had been plunged into her heart. "You don't mean that, Dad. We've disagreed before and allowed each other our space."

"This is different, Diana. You're going against the teachings of the Church, against our wishes, against society, against everything that is normal and good." He looked into her eyes. "If you insist on pursuing this, you are no longer our daughter!"

"I wish you didn't feel like that. Won't you at least meet Torrie?" Diana felt that she had to at least ask.

"Absolutely not!" he snapped. "And if you really have no intention of giving this up, you'd better leave this house now."

"You're putting me out?" Diana felt shock and disbelief. She couldn't believe this was really happening. "You're my parents. How could you do this?"

"Diana, your mother and I love you very much." Pain filled her father's eyes. "But we can't condone perversion. If you'd just reconsider, we'll do anything possible to help you get well and to save your career as a nun."

"There's nothing to reconsider, Dad. Torrie and I love each other. I plan to live with her as long as she'll have me."

"I'm very sorry you feel that way. You leave us no choice." There were tears in his eyes. "We no longer have a daughter."

Diana turned to her mother. "Do you feel the same way, Mom? Am I dead to you too?" Diana was heartbroken.

"I love you, Diana, but your father's right." Tears streamed down her mother's cheeks. "We'll pray for you."

They sat in stony silence on the way to the mother house. Her mother cried the whole way, and Diana stared out the window. When they reached the mother house, Diana's father parked the car at the front door of the main building.

"I won't change my mind." Diana felt a strong sense of finality. "I'll miss you both. Will you hug me good-bye and wish me luck?"

Neither parent moved. "We'll save the hugs and good wishes for the day you come to your senses and come home."

Diana swallowed the tears that filled her throat. "Okay. I guess all that's left is to say good-bye."

"Good-bye, Diana," her father said, staring ahead.

"Take care of yourself," her mother said through her tears.

Diana got out of the car, took her overnight case from the seat next to her, and walked to the door alone. She heard the car pull away, and turned to watch it. She brushed the tears from her eyes as she realized neither parent was looking back.

CHAPTER 25

Torrie's first morning at Johns Hopkins was filled with reexaminations and neurological tests. It was after two o'clock when she finally returned to her room. She had just about drifted off to sleep when a familiar voice awakened her.

"I can see you've taken to being a patient like a duck takes to water."

Torrie recognized her father's voice and opened her eyes to find her parents walking into her hospital room.

"I didn't expect you this early." She had

purposely down-played the nature of her hospitalization.

Her parents hugged her and kissed her on the cheek.

"The front line of the Redskins couldn't have kept your mother at home while you're right here at Johns Hopkins," Torrie's father said, adding a quick wink.

"Victor Lassiter, you were as anxious to see your daughter as I was," her mother said. Her mother pulled a chair closer to the bed and sat down. She held Torrie's hand. "Your father and I want the truth, dear. You don't check yourself into Johns Hopkins for tests you could have done in Atlanta."

The panic was rising inside her at the thought of telling her parents about her diagnosis, not to mention Diana. Her sexual orientation had never been discussed among them openly. Her parents had never directly asked, and she had never seen a reason to volunteer the information. But now her time was limited, and with the added opinions of the neurologists and neurosurgeons at Johns Hopkins, she felt that the truth, her truth, had to be told. Years of silence had built an invisible wall that locked such truth deep inside her. She wondered what kind of running start she would need to scale that wall, or to demolish it completely. A death sentence, she thought. It took a death sentence to make her willing to knock down the barricades and risk people's reactions to her. Would her parents still look at her with love and admiration? Would they still offer their full support?

"Torrie, I could just speak to your doctors." Her father was a physician too. "They'd tell me what they might not tell other parents in a similar situation." There was no threat in her father's voice, just concern and determination. "We'd rather hear it from you." He sat on the edge of Torrie's bed and rested his hand on her arm.

Her throat ached as she fought back the tears. She studied her parents and knew that what she was about to say would fill them with pain.

"I've given bad news to hundreds of patients." Torrie cleared her throat. "All of them put together weren't this hard." Her mother tightened her hold on her hand. Torrie looked at her father. "I have an inoperable brain tumor. I came up here to see if there was any way to treat it." She heard her mother's almost silent, "God, no," but kept her eyes focused on her father's face. His pale green eyes were veiled by a thin layer of tears. "They reviewed my records before I arrived, and did several more tests this morning. They gave me their findings this afternoon." She swallowed hard. "The tumor is a malignant glioma. It's located in the region of the optic chiasma." Torrie forced herself to face her mother. "There is no treatment, Mom."

Her mother closed her eyes for a moment, her face drained of color, but she never let go of Torrie's hand. When she looked at Torrie, her eyes were soft and filled with pain. "I'm so sorry, Torrie. So very sorry." She leaned over and wrapped her arms around her daughter. "My poor baby. I'd gladly change places with you if I could. Parents shouldn't outlive their children."

"Elizabeth." Victor Lassiter's voice was calm and solid. He put his hand on his wife's shoulder then handed her a clump of tissues from the box in the bedside table. "I can get some other people to take a look at you," he said to Torrie. "I'll find out what's the newest thing in research and get you into that program."

"Dad, I know you want to help, but it would be a waste of time. I'm not going into any experimental program. I'm not going into any kind of treatment." Torrie was resolved to keep control of her own life. "I'm satisfied that every option has been considered, and I choose to live the rest of my life with quality time. I'm not going to waste what time I have left in and out of hospitals."

"She's right, Victor." Her mother's voice was shaky, her words punctuated with sobs. "Torrie can come home and the three of us can travel like we did when she was growing up. We can go back to all the places Torrie liked best . . . England, Italy, Spain."

"Mom, I'm not moving back with you and Dad." Torrie spoke with all the love and tenderness she felt for her parents. "I'm going to lease my house in Atlanta and move to Saint Cloud."

"You shouldn't be alone. We can rent a house in Saint Cloud so we can be there for you when you need us."

"I appreciate the offer, Mom, but I won't be alone. I've been living with someone in Atlanta. We're very much in love, and whatever time I have left, we'll spend together."

"That's wonderful, dear." Her mother smiled through her tears. "Why didn't you tell us you were living with someone? Why didn't you bring him to meet us? Is he staying near here? We'd like to meet him. If he's that important to you, he's important to us."

"Maybe all four of us can go on a trip or two together." Her father's smile was obviously forced. "Your mother and I aren't exactly prudes. We realize young people today don't always wait for marriage to live together."

Torrie felt her heartbeat increase at the same moment she realized she was sweating. Once she told them, she wouldn't be able to take it back. They'd just learned that their only daughter was dying. Did they really need to know about Diana? She brushed her hand across her forehead. God, what was she thinking? This wasn't the time for lies and games.

"Mom, do you remember telling me about your sister? The one your family disowned?"

Her mother's expression became fluid, moving from confusion, to recognition, to shock, and back again to confusion. "What does Susan have to do with you? You've never even met her."

"I'd like to meet her," Torrie said. Keep going, she told herself. "You see, Mom, like Aunt Susan, the person I'm in love with is a woman."

Her mother's face froze halfway between recognition and shock.

"What are you saying, Torrie?" Victor Lassiter looked as if he were about to cry.

"That I'm a lesbian." Torrie felt as if a gigantic boulder had been lifted from her. "I've been attracted to women ever since I can remember. I never told you because I knew you would disapprove — that you might even disown me." Torrie felt some of the panic she had experienced as a child when she thought of talking to her parents about the way she felt about some of her girlfriends and some of her female teachers.

"My God!" her mother sputtered. "Not you too."

"I'd like you to meet Diana." Torrie hoped her parents reaction and final decision would surprise her. "She's a nurse practitioner. She's very bright, very tender, very spiritual."

Her mother looked ill.

"She was a nun. A missionary in Africa." Torrie watched them closely. "She's leaving the convent so we can be together."

"You're involved with a nun? A Catholic nun?"

"Yes, Dad," Torrie said.

Her father was incredulous. "Torrie, this could ruin your career."

Torrie began to laugh. "Dad, I'm dying. If the truth ruins my career, so be it." She laughed again. "What can they do to me?"

"Don't laugh, Torrie." Her mother was angry. "People will talk behind your back. They'll ridicule you. Tell dirty jokes about you and your friend. They'll say you seduced a nun."

"And they'd be partly right. We seduced each other."

There was a knock on the door and a nurse walked in. "I just have to get your vital signs, and I'll let you get back to your visitors."

Her mother jumped up. "We have to be going anyway." She walked toward her husband.

"Mom, wait," Torrie said. She turned to the nurse. "Could you come back in about thirty minutes?"

"Sure." The nurse put the thermometer away and left.

"How could you just walk off now?" Torrie asked.

"I have to know where you stand on this. Are you disowning me? Or am I still invited to bring my friend to your house? And are we still invited to take a trip or two with you?"

Shifting from one foot to the other as if deciding on which side of the question she would take her stand, her mother said, "Torrie, we love you very much, but we're too old-fashioned to accept our daughter with a lesbian lover. We'll do anything we can to help you — except socialize with you as a couple." She walked to the bed and kissed Torrie on the forehead. "You're welcome to come home at any time. But not with your lesbian lover."

Her father kissed Torrie on the cheek. "Please consider coming home so we can take care of you. You should be with your family at a time like this."

"Diana and I are family," Torrie said. "We're not just lovers. We're partners. Partners for life. Why won't you accept us? Why do you only think of us as lovers?"

"Because that's what you are," her mother said. "You make love together; that makes you lovers."

"But we're much more than that." Torrie tried to explain. "We love each other as individuals, and we want to share everything in our lives." She watched her mother's face. "We've worked together, played together, laughed together and cried together. We're two people who happen to be in love with each other. Sometimes we express our love by making love. But it isn't the most important part of our lives."

"Oh please, Torrie!" Her mother grimaced, and a quick, visible shiver went through her body. "I just hope I can get rid of the mental image of you two in bed with each other. It isn't pleasant to think of your daughter performing unnatural acts with some ex-nun."

Torrie was beginning to get angry. "That's totally unfair, Mom. You don't picture your heterosexual friends like that do you?"

"Of course not. Heterosexual sex is pretty much the same no matter who's involved. Besides, their lives are filled with lots of other things."

"So are mine and Diana's," Torrie said. "We're both individuals with full lives. Try thinking of us in some of those roles."

Her mother looked at Victor. He shrugged. "I guess it's only fair," he said.

She looked at Torrie. "Okay. I'll try." She pecked her on the forehead. "If you need anything, just let us know." She lifted Torrie's face upward and looked deeply into her eyes. "We are not disowning you. We love you. We're only refusing to socialize with you and your lover."

"Mom, you promised to try."

With a gesture that looked like surrender, she said, "Okay. You're right. I'll try."

"When are you going home?" her father asked.

"Diana should be here tomorrow. I'll be discharged in the morning," Torrie said. "We may spend a couple of days up here before we fly back to Atlanta."

"How about giving us a call when you get back home? Just to let us know how things are going."

"Sure, Dad," Torrie said. "I'll call as soon as we get back." She kissed him on the cheek. "Please give some thought to what we talked about. I'd really like to have your support, along with your love. I'd also like to know that you'd be here for Diana when I'm gone. It would mean a great deal to me."

"Give us time to think about it, Torrie."

CHAPTER 26

Sister Marie Angelos, the official doorkeeper, opened the door thirty seconds after Diana rang the bell. Sister Marie was dressed in the order's traditional habit, a custom observed, on a regular basis, by only the oldest nuns, and on special religious holidays, by the majority of the sisters. The bandeau, the stiff white cloth that covered Sister Marie's forehead, had cut an observable ridge across the thin skin of the elderly nun's tissue paper face. Her eyes and mouth crumpled into a smile. "Come in, come in," her frail voice whispered. "Reverend

Mother is expecting you in her office in an hour."
She started down a long hallway. "You'll have time
to settle in and freshen up before your meeting."

"Thank you." Diana forced a smile and followed
her to one of the private rooms used for visiting
dignitaries. She washed her face, stretched out on the
bed and thought about her vows.

She saw herself standing before the Reverend
Mother on the night before she took her first vows.
"Wear your habit proudly, Sister. It is a sign for all
that you are chosen by God for His own special
work." Mother Catherine's voice pealed like the bells
which called them to prayers.

The scene shifted only in the passage of time. She
was standing before Mother Catherine again. It was
the evening before her final vows. "It's only natural
to be frightened by the finality of the step you're
about to take, Sister." Mother Catherine looked
almost human for a moment. "But I can assure you
that this is a step God wills for you. We have
watched you closely in the six years since you first
received your habit. You are truly called and marked
by God to do his special work. Pronounce your
permanent vows boldly. It is God's will."

"It may have been at one time, Mother," Diana
murmured. "But God's plans and mine have changed
drastically."

An hour later Diana was seated in front of the
Reverend Mother's desk. The room was austere — a
plain wooden desk, wooden chairs, a single curtainless
window. A large graphic crucifix hung in a dark

corner over a rough, burgundy padded kneeler. It was exactly as she remembered it.

"Come in, my child," Reverend Mother invited from behind her desk. "Make yourself comfortable and tell me what's troubling you. You sounded very distressed when you called." She smiled. "Whatever the problem, I'm sure we can work it out."

"We can't work this out, Reverend Mother." Her heart raced as she continued. "I've come to ask that I be released from my vows. I'm leaving the order immediately."

The Mother General looked as if she had just been hit by a bucket of cold water. Her face was almost as white as the bandeau that covered her forehead. "Leaving? But you're going to Kenya in two weeks. It's exactly what you always said you wanted."

"It *was* what I wanted." She forced herself to go on. "My life has changed radically. I'm in love and we want to spend as much time as possible together. The person is terminally ill, so every day matters."

"Fallen in love with an individual? A mere man . . . ?" Her eyes opened wider, and her voice pitched two octaves higher. "You'd give up God for a man?"

She took a deep breath and looked directly at the Mother General. Her long face and pale gray eyes gave her an unearthly appearance.

"Not for a man, Reverend Mother — for a woman. I'm in love with a woman and we plan to spend our lives together."

Reverend Mother's face turned a whiter shade of pale, and her mouth dropped open. For twenty seconds she said nothing, then deep guttural sounds formed themselves into words. "Do you know what you're saying? ... Do you realize you will forfeit your soul if you follow this course? — That you will have separated yourself from the Church entirely?"

She knew better than the Reverend Mother what the impact of her actions would be concerning the order and the Church. "I've meditated about it for many days. I'm completely aware of the consequences." She pulled a large envelope from her brown leather shoulder bag and placed it on the desk. "I'm returning the airline tickets and the check for a thousand dollars."

"I beg you to reconsider this course. If you become involved with this woman, your soul will be damned to hell." Reverend Mother looked physically ill.

"I'm already involved with her, and I don't intend to give her up."

"Let us at least get you a psychiatrist — maybe he can bring you to your senses."

Diana was insulted and angry. "I've heard all I intend to listen to about losing my sanity and my soul." She stood, pulled the gold wedding band from her left hand and placed it on the desk next to the airline tickets. "Can someone drive me to the airport, or should I call a taxi?"

"Given what you've told me, I'm not willing to endanger one of my nuns by putting her in your presence. You'll need to call a taxi."

"Fine. May I sign the form requesting release from my vows?"

Reverend Mother's face was filled with contempt as she reached into the bottom desk drawer and placed the release form in front of Diana. She looked at her directly. "Let me make sure I understand what you've told me — you have already been sexually intimate with this woman."

Diana continued filling out the brief form, signed her name, and replaced her pen in her bag, then looked at the Mother General. She could feel the hatred and disdain in the old nun's eyes. Diana was determined to avoid pretense. "That's correct, Mother. We have already been intimate."

The Mother General sprang out of her chair and all but ran to the door. "Don't call me Mother. You've lost that right." She opened the door to her office. "Just call a cab, get your things, and leave these holy grounds."

As Diana walked out of her office, the Reverend Mother called after her, "And may God have mercy on your soul."

CHAPTER 27

There was a knock on the door and Torrie looked up from the *New York Times*. "Come in," she called. "You certainly sound as strong as a horse." Megan McKenzie strode into Torrie's hospital room.

"Megan, what are you doing in Baltimore? Don't tell me you have patients up here."

"No. No patients," Megan McKenzie said. "Just a very good friend and a three day cardiovascular conference." She embraced Torrie and kissed her on the cheek. "Besides, my sister lives up here. Why didn't you tell me what was happening?"

"I wanted to see how things turned out first."
Torrie felt slightly guilty. She probably should have
told her. "I'm sorry, Meggie. Things happened so fast,
I guess I just didn't think."

"I understand." Megan sat down on Torrie's bed.
"What have you found out?"

Torrie felt the weight of her bad news each time
she told it. She watched Megan's face as she
explained the whole story. There were tears in
Megan's eyes.

"Is there anything I can do, Torrie? Any way I
can help?"

"Not unless you have some special kind of magic
that works with parents. I told mine about Diana. It
seems they can't get rid of the picture of the two of
us in bed performing 'unnatural acts.' "

Megan patted her shoulder. "I'm afraid that's true
in nine out of ten cases. Parents seem to have a
hard time accepting their children as total and
complete individuals. Once they hear the word
lesbian, or the word *lover,* all they can think about is
the two people in bed, as lesbian lovers."

"Even if we couldn't make love anymore, I'd love
Diana just as much as I love her now."

"Of course you would," Megan said. "But most
people never think of that."

"And how does one get parents to see the truth?"

"It's pretty much up to them. Some parents come
around. Some never do."

"That isn't exactly what I wanted to hear," Torrie
said.

"How's Diana taking the situation?"

"She's doing okay. In fact, she'll be here in the

morning when I'm discharged. I've wanted you two to meet each other for a long time."

"Yes, but perhaps under different circumstances," Megan said.

"The three of us will get together back in Atlanta."

Torrie filled Megan in on what Diana had told her when she called from the Buffalo Airport.

"It sounds as if reality has hit her pretty hard. Perhaps you two could spend a couple of days in Baltimore."

"We've already planned to do that. In fact Diana is flying in late tonight and will get a suite at the Hilton for us."

The next morning, Diana drove directly to the hotel. "Are you sure you don't want to stop and get something to eat?" Diana asked as she parked the car.

"I'm positive," Torrie said. "I just want to be alone with you."

Diana smiled. "I like that idea a lot."

As the elevator carried them to the ninth floor, Torrie couldn't take her eyes off Diana. She had only one thought: to make love with her once they were alone.

The room was painted hotel-white, with white sectional furniture situated to form a conversational grouping around the gas-log fireplace. A large white fake fur throw rug covered the area in front of the fireplace.

"Would you like something to drink?" Diana asked. "They have the refrigerator well stocked."

"I don't care for anything," Torrie said. "Unless you count wanting to make love to you."

"That counts." She put her arms around Torrie and opened her mouth to Torrie's kiss.

Torrie felt the heat of passion move through her body.

"Do you want to go into the bedroom?" Diana asked in a husky whisper as Torrie's hand moved between her thighs.

"No," Torrie said. She covered Diana's mouth with hot insistent kisses. "Let's make love here, in front of the fireplace."

Torrie's excitement doubled as she pulled off Diana's sweater, dropped it on the floor and bent to take Diana's breast into her mouth. "I love you, Diana."

They undressed each other and lay naked against the soft, white fur rug.

Torrie lay beside Diana and trailed her fingertips like a paintbrush across Diana's face and lips, around the curve of her shoulder, to her breast, downward to the hot, wet vee between her thighs. Torrie slowly spread the hot, wet lips, caressing the silken folds that opened willingly to reveal the firm, pink pearl that awaited Torrie's touch.

Diana shuddered as Torrie entered her and moved deep into the hot, warm darkness that closed around her. She sucked Diana's nipple firmly between her teeth, stroking it again and again with her tongue.

Diana grasped Torrie's back then guided her head downward. Torrie deposited hot kisses along Diana's abdomen and down the front of her thighs. Her mouth was on fire as she moved to Diana's inner thighs and trailed upward to the pearl.

Diana moaned and pushed Torrie's head closer to herself.

Torrie inhaled the sweet musky fragrance and exhaled against the firmness of the pearl. Torrie's own passion grew as she sucked the pearl and silken lips inside.

"Oh, Torrie!" Diana called in a dreamlike voice.

Torrie increased the intensity of her strokes and sucked Diana deeper into her mouth. Diana arched her hips upward, pressing herself more firmly against Torrie's mouth. Torrie's passion burst and her strokes became harder and faster. She was lost inside her own desire. Suddenly she was spinning wildly. Diana's voice was all around her, Diana's murmured ecstasy, Diana's scream of ultimate delight. Torrie felt herself drawn in an upward spiral, moving ever higher in a crescendo of intimate pleasure.

Spent and satisfied, they lay in each others arms.

"I love you, Diana," Torrie whispered. "I wanted you so badly. To feel you against my skin, taste you in my mouth, feel myself deep inside you." Torrie looked into Diana's eyes. "I had to remind myself that I'm still very much alive. Still able to touch and be touched."

Diana tightened her arms around Torrie and pressed her mouth firmly against Torrie's. "Make love to me again," she said. "I want you."

CHAPTER 28

When they arrived back in Atlanta, there was a letter from the mother house. Diana skimmed it quickly. "It looks like the Reverend Mother has forgone her Christian charity." She folded the letter. "To say that I'm persona non grata . . . is to put it mildly. My 'wickedness' is to blame for everything from the Spanish Inquisition to the decline of the Vatican's influence in America. So it seems. I never realized before how much I individually affect Vatican and world relations."

"I feel sorry for the Reverend Mother," Torrie

said. "She has no idea what being in love really means. I'm not sure whether to hope that she discovers that chastity is its own punishment, or just wish her love. In any event you're not persona non grata here and you won't be in Saint Cloud." She put her arm around Diana's shoulder. "We have a lot of packing to do, so let's forget the past and look toward our future."

"You're right." Diana smiled and changed the subject. "It was nice of Anne to agree to lease the house for a year, and nice of Megan to put the deal together with her friend. I'm glad she had a friend in need of a house."

Diana put the final piece of masking tape on a box of towels and linens she had just finished packing.

"Yes, it was," Torrie said. She pushed the boxes aside, sat down on the floor and rested her back against the sofa. "It won't be like leaving the house with strangers." She pulled Diana gently down beside her. "We both need a break."

Diana yielded, placing her head against Torrie's shoulder. The living room was already stacked with boxes, and there was a lot more to pack. "It looks more like a warehouse every time I look around."

Torrie kissed Diana on the nose. "Well it won't look like a warehouse for long." As if to add his own form of encouragement, Winston climbed onto Diana's lap and began to lick her face. "See," Torrie said. "Winston agrees with me." Torrie looked happy. "In a few days Saint Cloud will seem as if it's always been our home. I like that thought — our home."

"So do I," Diana said. She looked at Torrie and remembered the taste of Torrie's mouth against her own. It never ceased to amaze her. She could make love with Torrie at any hour of the day or night; there was always something new to discover. She reached up and pulled Torrie toward her. Their lips met, and each sought the warm, dark mystery of the other with her kiss. Diana could feel desire growing between her thighs. "Make love to me," she whispered.

Torrie's hand beneath her shirt felt hot and soft against her skin.

Diana slipped her hands beneath Torrie's sweater and felt her shudder.

The sound of the doorbell broke their growing desire.

"Ignore it," Diana whispered. She undid Torrie's bra and caressed the fullness of her breasts. Her anticipation doubled as she felt Torrie's nipples stiffen in response to her touch.

The bell rang again, followed by a dull pounding on the door. A familiar voice, muffled but recognizable, called, "Diana? Are you in there? Diana!"

Diana felt as if someone had plunged her into a tub of ice water. She withdrew her hands and sat bolt upright. "My God!" she gasped. "It's my brother! What's he doing here?"

"Shouldn't we invite him in and find out?" Torrie sounded serious, but her expression was one of amusement. "It certainly isn't polite to leave him standing on the front steps."

Diana scrambled to her feet and smoothed her sweater and her slacks. She looked at Torrie. "Please don't leave me alone with him."

"That might be difficult, Diana. I'm sure he'll want to talk with you privately."

Diana panicked at the thought. "Torrie, I don't think I can take another emotional beating right now. My parents probably sent him."

Torrie stood up and put her arms around Diana. "I'm with you all the way. You're not alone." The doorbell rang again. "We'd better let him in."

Diana took a deep breath and opened the door. Her brother was smiling down at her.

"Peter. It's good to see you. You look wonderful. I'm not sure I would have recognized you on the street." She hugged him. "You look positively handsome in the uniform."

"Thank you." Peter took a step back and looked at her. "And you look positively beautiful without your uniform!" He followed her into the living room. "It's been so long since I saw you without your habit that I'd almost forgotten how beautiful you are."

"Peter, this is my friend, Torrie Lassiter. I'm sure Mom and Dad have mentioned her to you."

"They certainly have." Peter extended his hand. "It's nice to meet you, Doctor. Thank you for having me in your home."

"As Diana's brother, you're always welcome." Torrie gestured toward the sofa, "Won't you sit down? I was about to make coffee. Would you like a cup?"

Peter relaxed on the sofa and placed his hat on the end table. "I'd love a cup." He looked at the stacks of boxes. "It looks as if I almost missed you."

Diana watched him closely. He looked friendly and happy. Not at all like a son who had come to talk some sense into a wayward sister's head. Diana hoped her confusion didn't show.

"We're leaving for Saint Cloud tomorrow," she said. Why didn't he just say why he'd come, she wondered. Her stomach felt as if some unseen hands had tied it into a gigantic knot. She was more nervous facing Peter than she was facing her parents or facing the Reverend Mother. But Peter had always been the perfect big brother. Until he announced that he was not going into the priesthood, their parents had spoken of Peter as if he were the perfect genetic specimen. At that point, their parents seemed to pin their hopes on Diana. She wondered if her parents would still have disowned her if Peter had been a priest. Of course they would have, she told herself. A priest couldn't have a sister who was in love with a woman.

Torrie returned with a tray and placed a mug of coffee before each of them. For almost a minute, everyone's attention seemed focused on the coffee. Diana looked at Torrie, saw her smile and remembered she was not alone.

"Peter, I'm not exactly sure what Mom and Dad told you, but I think you should know that I have no intention of changing my mind or my heart. So if that's why you're here, you're wasting your time."

Peter set down his mug. "I didn't come here to change your mind. But you're right. Mom and Dad asked me to do just that."

"Then why did you come?" Diana asked, confused.

"I wanted to offer you and your friend my support. If there's anything I can do to help you in any way, all you have to do is ask."

Diana was surprised. "Peter, are you certain you understood the relationship between Torrie and me?"

"I think so." He shrugged. "You and Torrie are in love with each other and intend to spend the rest of your lives together. Is that about right?"

"Yes," Diana said. A glimmer of hope lit a small corner of her heart. "It's the reason Mom and Dad disowned me."

"I don't think anything or anybody could change their minds." Peter looked serious. "They have no idea of what a real gay relationship is about. The little bit they think they know is completely negative. They'd be easier to talk to if they'd just admit they don't know anything. At least then one could begin on an even playing field with them, instead of ten steps down."

"But you do understand?" Diana was still wary of Peter's motives. "Forgive me if I seem cautious, Peter. In the past week, I've learned that most people I thought really cared about me could care less once they found out I'm in love with a woman. I'd like to believe that you accepted me and understood my feelings, but from what I know about you, it just doesn't add up."

Peter's face lit up, and he smiled. "That's because you're missing an important piece of information. I've known I was gay since I was fourteen. That's one of the reasons I didn't want to become a priest."

Diana's jaw dropped and she stared at him. This has to be a dream, she thought. How could he be gay? How could he have hidden it so well?

"Diana." Peter's voice brought Diana back to the present. "You look as if you're going to faint." He laughed. "I didn't mean to shock you. I thought you'd be happy to know that I do understand what you're going through, and that I support you one hundred percent."

"I am happy," Diana said. "It's wonderful that you really understand. I can't even express how much I appreciate your telling me. It must have taken a lot of courage to come here." Diana was amused at her reaction. "I'm just shocked. I never suspected it."

"Well, I never thought about you as gay either. I almost passed out when Mom and Dad told me they wanted me to talk to you about the woman you were living with, the woman you had left the convent for." He smiled at Torrie. "I guess you and I are in-laws."

Torrie laughed. "Well, it's one of the nicer things I've been told in the past week." She looked at Diana. "I'm glad you'll have some support. It will be even more important in the future."

Diana felt suddenly overcome by sadness. "Torrie, please don't talk about this now. I'm not sure I can handle it."

Torrie took Diana's hand. "We'll handle it together. Besides, I'm not talking about tomorrow or next week. We'll have lots of time together."

Diana brushed a tear from her cheek. She looked at Peter. "Did Mom and Dad tell you that Torrie is seriously ill? I'm not even sure they heard me when I brought it up."

"They told me your friend had AIDS," he said. "I figured they had gotten whatever you said mixed up." He looked at Torrie. "Are you ill?"

As Torrie explained her condition, Diana wished she could take her into her arms and somehow make what she was saying untrue. She wondered if hearing the words would always tear into her heart like broken glass.

"I'm sorry," Peter said. "I didn't know how serious it was. I hope I'm not intruding by coming here tonight."

"You're welcome here. I like the idea of finally meeting someone who can tell me what Diana was like as a child. You'll always be welcome in our home."

"Thank you," Peter said. He turned toward Diana. "You didn't know I was gay because I didn't want anyone to know. I was afraid Mom and Dad would disown me. I was also afraid I'd lose you. It seems strange that the thing I felt might drive us apart is precisely what's brought us closer together. I hope the three of us can be good friends."

"Well, you can start by telling us about yourself," Diana said, curious about him. "Are you seeing someone?"

"I've been involved with the same man for three years," Peter said. "Unfortunately, I'm stationed here and he's stationed in San Antonio, so we don't see each other very often. We go on leave together, and once in a while we manage a long weekend."

"So your friend is in the Army too?" Diana said.

"Yes. He's a colonel. He's very fearful of being found out and drummed out of the Army. But I think that may change a little now."

"Why is that?" Diana asked.

"I just don't think I'll ever feel the same about being gay and hiding it from everyone again." Peter's dark brown eyes looked warm and tender. "When Mom and Dad told me about you, I was impressed. It made me feel somewhat cowardly to find out that my

157

kid sister had stood up to them and I still couldn't find the courage to do the same."

"I didn't really have a choice. I knew I wanted to live with Torrie, and that meant leaving the convent." Diana shrugged. "Also, I didn't want to have to lie about who I am, who I love. We don't have time for games. There's no such thing as telling one lie. Every lie leads to other lies. We want to make every minute count. There's no room for pretense."

"That's exactly what I meant. You're living the life you choose to live." Peter was suddenly teary-eyed. "You seem so perfect together. I'm so sorry you got such a rotten break."

Diana took Torrie's hand and held it tightly. "Don't feel sorry for us, Peter. We're very much in love and whatever time we have together will be loving and caring. That's a lot more than most people experience in years and years together."

"You're right," Peter said. "You two have something I want in my own life. I think I'll talk to Michael. We can at least start making plans for life after the military." He looked at his watch. "I'd better be going. I have the duty in the morning." He stood up. "How about a hug?"

Diana hugged him. "I'm glad you came. I hope you'll visit us in Saint Cloud."

"Count on it." He looked at Torrie. "I think Diana is lucky to have you." He stepped between them and put his arms around their shoulders. "You're lucky to have each other."

"I'm looking forward to your next visit," Torrie said. "You're the first blood relation to accept us as a couple. I'm so glad you'll be there for Diana."

"I'll be there for both of you," Peter said. "Don't you forget that."

"Thank you. I appreciate that," Torrie said. They walked him to the door.

"Peter," Diana said. "What are you going to tell Mom and Dad?"

"That I think you've chosen the better part of life. The part filled with love and genuine caring."

"They won't like that." She chuckled. "If they hated having one gay child, they sure won't like having two."

"No, they won't," Peter said. "But it's about time they learned to live with the truth."

"It won't change them, you know," Diana said.

"No, it won't," Peter said. "But it's already changed me."

CHAPTER 29

"Do you hear me? Feed me or I'm quitting," Lynn Bradley called up the stairs.

Diana pushed two empty cartons into the hallway and looked down at Lynn. "Don't you dare quit. I'll be right down to make sandwiches. Let me get Torrie first or she'll just go on working."

"Ah, yes!" Lynn said. "Our friend, the workaholic. I'll help you separate her from her unpacking."

Lynn bounded up the stairs. Her faded blue jeans and light blue t-shirt accented her tall, slender body and flat stomach. Lynn and Megan had proven to be good friends to Diana as well as to Torrie.

Lynn pushed two empty boxes to the side. "I'll take the boxes away from her. You drag her downstairs."

"It's a deal," Diana said. She liked Lynn's sense of humor.

"Okay, Torrie," Lynn said as she opened the bedroom door. "No more unpacking for a while. It's time to feed your slave labor."

Lynn and Diana stopped just inside the door. Torrie was lying on the bed, a white washcloth covering her eyes. Winston was lying on the pillow next to her.

"Torrie, are you all right?" Diana rushed to Torrie's side.

"I'm fine," Torrie said. "It's just a headache. A plain, ordinary headache."

"Is there anything we can do?" Diana asked. "Would you like something to drink?"

"Diana, I'll be fine. I've already taken something. In fact, I'm starting to get drowsy. If I can sleep for a couple of hours, I'll be fine. You two go ahead and eat. I'll eat when I wake up." She squeezed Diana's hand. "Don't let me sleep longer than two hours or I won't be able to sleep tonight."

"All right," Diana said. "I'll leave the door open. Call if you want anything."

"I will," Torrie said. "Now get out of here and let me rest."

Diana exchanged glances with Lynn and they both went down to the kitchen and prepared lunch.

They ate in the living room, exchanging small talk until their second cup of coffee.

Diana fought to control her anxiety concerning Torrie. Her worst fears were creeping into her mind. What if the doctors were wrong about how much time Torrie had left?

Diana looked up to find Lynn staring at her.

"Lynn, I know this will sound silly, but I can't stop worrying about it. The thought that she'll die and I won't be there with her terrifies me. What if this headache is . . ." Diana couldn't bring herself to finish.

"Is the warning sign, and death only hours away?" Lynn finished the thought for her.

God, I hate those words, Diana thought. Maybe it was better not to talk about it.

"Diana, it's all right to talk about your fears," Lynn said softly. "In fact, it's healthy."

Could Lynn read her mind? Maybe it would help to talk. "I'm afraid Torrie will need me and I won't be there," Diana said. "I'm afraid I'll fail her."

"I don't think that will happen," Lynn said. "Torrie's last headache will be unmistakably different. Torrie will know. And given the way Torrie feels about you, if she knows, you'll know."

"I hate being helpless," Diana said. She wiped tears from her cheeks. "It's so hard to look at her and know that I only have her for a little while. I can't even imagine my life without her. I can't imagine any future that doesn't include Torrie." She met Lynn's eyes. "Sometimes I think it would be better if I died when Torrie dies. It would spare me the pain of being left without her."

"Have you talked to Torrie about your feelings?" Lynn asked.

"No, I don't want to add to her problems. She

has enough to deal with just living with her diagnosis."

"You're living with her diagnosis too, Diana. In a way, Torrie is luckier than you are."

Diana was shocked. "How can you say such a thing?"

"Because Torrie won't be the one left behind. She won't be the one left standing in the middle of the rubble of her former life. And she won't be the one who has to face family and friends if someone decides to challenge the will."

The weight of Lynn's words sank in.

"Torrie didn't have to change her life as drastically as you did," Lynn continued. "Leaving the convent must have been very difficult for you. Not to mention being disowned by your parents and your order."

Lynn's words slammed into Diana like arrows piercing the center of a bull's-eye. Diana recognized the truth she had been avoiding.

"Your life as you knew it before you met Torrie is virtually in shambles. And when Torrie dies, the realities of the world you turned upside down will hit you."

"If you're trying to scare me, you're succeeding," Diana said. "But it isn't the first time I've faced the facts. I know what I've chosen, and I'd choose it again, if it meant being with Torrie. Whatever the consequences are, they won't outweigh my time with Torrie. I'd trade the rest of my life for just one more year, one more month, one more week, with her." Diana wiped the tears from her face and took a deep breath. "I'm where I want to be, and I wouldn't have it any other way."

"She's a very lucky woman," Lynn said. "You're both blessed." Lynn reached out and took Diana's hand. "I'll help in any way I can, in any way you'll allow."

"Thank you, Lynn. I really appreciate your concern and your friendship. It's good to know you're here."

CHAPTER 30

"They're here!" Torrie called. "I knew they'd be early."

Diana hurried across the room and placed two trays of hors d'oeuvres on the large, square cherry wood coffee table in front of the sofa.

"She looks like my mother," Torrie said. "Younger, but anyone could tell they're related."

"Well, stop looking at them through the window and let them in." Diana said.

Torrie opened the door just as her aunt pressed the bell.

"Aunt Susan," Torrie said. She couldn't take her eyes off the tall silver-haired woman.

"It's so good to finally meet you, Torrie," Susan O'Keefe said. She stepped forward and wrapped her arms around her niece.

Torrie felt her anxiety about their meeting melting away with her aunt's embrace. It was as if she had known this woman all her life.

"Oh, excuse me." Susan turned to the gray-haired, petite woman next to her. "This is my partner, Joyce Branson. Joyce teaches English literature at the University of Chicago."

Torrie extended her hand. "I'm glad you were able to come." She introduced Diana. The four exchanged amenities then settled on the sofa and chairs in front of the fireplace.

"This is a beautiful room," Joyce said. She looked up at the stained glass window Torrie and Diana had bought at a local antique shop. "That window is absolutely perfect in this room."

"Thank you," Diana said. "We feel the same way."

"The dove looks as if it could take flight any second," Susan said. "I don't believe I've ever seen anything like it." She looked at Diana. "I don't suppose it had a double or a mate that might still be available?"

"I'm afraid not," Diana said. "It's truly one of a kind, like your niece."

"My niece." Susan turned to Torrie. "You have no idea how many times I thought about you, about taking you for boat rides on the lake, to the zoo, or giving you advice on college or medical school."

"I'm afraid Mother kept you her secret," Torrie said. "When I was a child, I thought you must have done something really awful to be disowned by the family. It wasn't until I was eighteen that I overheard Mother talking to Dad about you and your lesbian lover."

"My lesbian lover," Susan said as if talking to herself. She took Joyce's hand. "Your mother never understood that being in love with a woman involved much more than making love together. Joyce and I had been together more than ten years at that time and I thought . . . no that's wrong, I *hoped* that our years together would help her understand that our relationship was a matter of love. I explained that we had been there for each other through good times and bad. That she had helped me stay in medical school the two or three times I'd wanted to quit, and I had helped her stay in the doctoral program when it seemed there was no end to the obstacles between her and her Ph.D."

Susan smiled at Joyce then continued. "Elizabeth's mind was shut up as tight as a submarine. She wrote me a letter encouraging me to give up my 'sinful' life and join the world of the morally correct and happy heterosexuals — 'moral people,' she called them." She took a deep breath. "I wrote her once or twice after that, but she never responded. I finally lost hope and gave up trying to make peace with her."

"That sounds like Mother," Torrie said. "I'm afraid she hasn't changed a great deal on the subject. The only ray of hope came in a phone call last week. She called to say that she and Dad would 'drop by' on Christmas Eve, on their way to visit friends for Christmas." Torrie paused, and smiled to herself, remembering her mother's explanation. "They want to drop off presents for both of us. That's quite a step for her. She hasn't exactly done a one-eighty-degree turn, but at least she recognizes Diana's existence. It'll be interesting."

" 'Interesting' is an understatement," Susan said. "I'd love to be the proverbial fly on the wall for that visit."

"I'll let you know what happens," Torrie said. "I'm rather dreading it. I just hope she doesn't get back on the convert-or-be-disowned kick."

"I don't think they'd come all the way to Saint Cloud to do that," Diana said. "They could have done it over the phone. I think they're really trying to make peace with you."

Torrie shrugged. "I guess so."

"Diana is probably right," Susan said. "No matter what your mother says, I know she loves you a great deal. Those feelings are even stronger than her fears."

"It didn't work that way for you," Torrie said.

"No, but I'm her sister, not her child. And she most likely feels she has unlimited time with me for reconciliation. Since she knows about your health, she also knows that your time is very precious."

"Susan, that sounds so callous. Very medical," Joyce said, frowning.

"Lord, Joyce," Susan said. "Torrie's a physician. She knows the facts of her case better than anyone." She turned to Torrie. "I'm sorry if I seemed callous. I certainly don't feel that way toward you."

Torrie was touched. "I understand, and I appreciate your concern. You're right about Mother's being affected by my diagnosis. I'll never forget the look on her face when I told her."

"I can imagine," Susan said. "I know how I felt

when you told me. And I know that no matter how hard it is for me and your mother, it must be a hundred times worse for you and Diana. If there is anything we can do . . . anything . . . all you have to do is ask."

Torrie swallowed the tears she felt rising in her throat. "I appreciate that. I think Diana and I have most of the bases covered." She raised Diana's hand and kissed the back of her fingers. "One thing I will ask is that you be there for Diana later." Torrie glanced at Diana and smiled. "Ex-nuns aren't used to asking for emotional support. They're also not as tough as they like to think. It would mean a great deal to me to know that Diana will be accepted as family by you two."

"Of course," Susan said. She looked at Diana. "You'll always have a home in Chicago. You're welcome anytime."

"Thank you," Diana said. "Your emotional support means a lot."

"It's not just emotional support, Diana," Joyce said. "You're like a niece to us. Susan and I have spent hours talking about all the things we would liked to have done with Torrie, and for Torrie, if we could have been part of her life when she was growing up. We look forward to whatever part we can play in your lives now . . . and in the future."

Diana wiped two or three escaped tears from her cheek. "I hope we can visit you in Chicago in the early part of next year. I've never been there."

Joyce said, "We'll look forward to it."

Torrie felt relief and sadness. It was wonderful to know that her relationship, and Diana, were accepted, yet she prayed she would live to make the trip.

* * * * *

It was three AM when Torrie slipped out of bed and tiptoed to the deck off her bedroom. Her head had started throbbing an hour earlier and the pain had grown steadily worse. She sat on the swing and swallowed two fifty-milligram tablets of Demerol with some water.

The cold air felt good. Like an ice bag on her head, she thought, only better, because the "ice bag" came with a cool breeze. She sat back in the swing and closed her eyes. The two days of her aunt's visit had been reassuring. In many ways, she and Susan were a lot alike. She couldn't help but wonder how things might have been different when she was growing up if she had known her.

A sharp pain shot through her head and for a few seconds, she felt dizzy. Her heart was pounding as she looked from the sky to the deck, checking to make sure her vision wasn't affected. She could feel the small beads of sweat on her forehead. She hated being afraid. What was she afraid of? Dying? She didn't think so. She just didn't want to die without a chance to tell Diana everything she wanted her to know.

Lord, she prayed, *if you really do listen to and answer prayers, please grant me enough time to say a proper good-bye to Diana. Enough time to make sure she'll have the emotional support she'll need, and the financial resources to spend her life in the way that will make her the most happy. I guess I haven't prayed since I was a child. I read somewhere that it's the stranger's voice that stands out in a crowd. That being the case, Lord, you certainly can't miss my requests. And that being the case, Lord, I hope you'll give me whatever strength I need to die with dignity, and to leave Diana with good memories. I do love her. I will always love her. If there's an immortal soul, I don't want mine to ever forget the love I feel for her. And when the time comes for her to leave this life, please let us recognize each other in whatever place souls go to wait for those they love and left behind.*

Torrie felt herself getting sleepy, and her head hurt less. She stood up and crept back to bed. She pressed her body against Diana's and drifted off to sleep.

CHAPTER 31

Diana watched the helicopter become a dark spot against the clear blue sky as it moved farther and farther from the island.

"You look a little pale," Torrie said. "You're not having second thoughts, are you?"

Diana looked at her. Her mint green, short-sleeved sweatshirt and shorts looked cool against the bright sunlight and sun-bleached sand. "No second thoughts," Diana said. "I've just never been dropped off on an island by a helicopter before." She smiled.

"Not that I'm complaining, mind you. I like being marooned with you."

"Semi-marooned," Torrie said. "We're only thirty minutes from the Florida Keys. One call on the shortwave radio, and a helicopter will be here in half an hour to carry us back to civilization."

"Well, we're as marooned as we'll probably ever get," Diana said.

The white two-story house was about one hundred and fifty yards from the beach. The rolling dunes varied from golden to white in color. The tide was in, and waves were breaking hard against the beach. They left lacy, white pools behind as they receded back to the dark blue ocean.

"It's beautiful here. I still can't believe our luck in getting this paradise to ourselves for five whole days." She reached for Torrie's hand. "Where else could I walk with you hand-in-hand but on our own private island?"

"Doctor McKenzie's private island." Torrie corrected her. "She and Lynn apparently spend a lot of time here. It's too bad they had to work over Thanksgiving." She put her arm around Diana's shoulders. "But I'm glad they offered it to us."

They walked in silence for a few minutes. Diana watched Winston run toward the incoming waves, stop dead in his tracks, bark at the white foam, then turn and chase the foam inland. He sent one last bark in the direction of the dissolving foam, then turned to begin the process again.

"I think he's enjoying himself," Diana said. "I think he's grinning." Diana felt totally alive. The weight of Torrie's arm on her shoulders, the scent of her cologne, the salty taste of the fine ocean mist, the sound of waves, the screeching gulls — all contributed to her exquisite sense of union with nature.

"I hope you were telling the truth when you said you make a terrific turkey dinner and trimmings." She stopped and looked at Torrie. "I'd be awfully disappointed if our Thanksgiving dinner for tomorrow got burned up in the oven. We don't have a backup turkey, you know."

"We don't need a 'backup turkey,'" Torrie said. "You're not the only good cook in this family. I bet I could teach you a thing or two in the kitchen."

Diana felt drawn to Torrie like an incoming tide to a welcoming beach. She felt her stomach muscles tighten and remembered how soft Torrie's skin felt against her own. "Is that right?" she asked, giving her a kiss. "You taste like salt." She ran her tongue slowly across Torrie's lips. "You taste like summer."

Torrie's arms closed around her and Diana was aware of each curve, hollow, and swell of Torrie's body. She opened her mouth willingly to receive Torrie's tongue. It moved slowly inside her mouth, calling Diana's passions to the surface, fanning their flames as they leapt toward her.

"Let's forget about cooking tonight," Torrie whispered against Diana's mouth.

They began walking toward the house. Suddenly a fast-moving ball of fur shot by them and leaped for a cloud of sea foam — without success. "Might as well give up for now, Winston," Diana said. "Tomorrow is another day."

Winston slowed down as if he understood, and sauntered the rest of the way to the house just ahead of his favorite people.

"Who ever heard of a picnic on Thanksgiving Day?" Torrie carried the picnic basket Diana had packed, plus two large canvas bags, one over each shoulder. "I feel like a pack mule. It's almost two o'clock and I'm starving. When do we eat?"

"Soon, soon," Diana said. The tide was out so they walked a little closer to the water's edge. Torrie's face was filled with color left by the sun and wind of yesterday. She looked perfectly happy and wonderfully healthy, Diana thought. Maybe the doctors were wrong. The thought flew through Diana's mind and was gone as quickly as it appeared.

They walked for several minutes. "Okay, stop here," Diana said. "Help me spread the tablecloth and beach towels out."

"I'm glad you thought of beach towels to sit on," Torrie said. "I hate to get sand in my clothes."

The ten-pound turkey Torrie cooked that morning was perfectly brown and could have served as a model for a November magazine cover.

"Well, what do you think? Wouldn't you say this was worth waiting for?" Diana asked.

"It looks terrific!" Torrie said. "But before we eat, I have a surprise."

"I thought you were starving." Diana sat back on her heels and put her hands on her hips.

"All things in time. This is important." Torrie opened one of the large bags and pulled out a small ice chest, two white linen napkins, a bottle of champagne and two napkin-wrapped, crystal champagne glasses.

"Our first Thanksgiving calls for a toast." She peeled the foil from the bottle and pushed the cork outward with both thumbs. There was a loud pop and champagne cascaded down the neck of the bottle. "Glasses, Nurse," Torrie ordered.

"Yes, Doctor." Diana held both glasses while Torrie filled them and set the open bottle upright in the ice chest.

"I want to make a toast to us: to our first Thanksgiving, and our first Thanksgiving Day picnic on the beach!" Torrie tapped her glass against Diana's. "To you, to me, to us. Forever!"

"To us. Forever!" Diana repeated. They both took a sip of champagne, then Diana lifted her glass in a sign of another toast. "A salute to Dr. Lassiter, who never ceases to surprise, amaze and delight me."

Desire growing inside her, Diana clicked her glass against Torrie's. "I love you, Torrie Lassiter. More than words can ever express." She sipped from her glass. "I've always wondered what it would be like to drink champagne from mouth to mouth." She took another sip, then kissed Torrie. She sat back, giggling.

Torrie drained her glass, then took Diana in her arms.

Diana opened her mouth as Torrie's lips grazed her own. Her heart pounded as Torrie showered her with kisses, long, tender kisses. Fires that moved through her body like molten rivers, filled her with passion, directing the force of her desire.

Torrie caressed her breast and squeezed her nipples between her fingers.

Diana was spinning with the heat of Torrie's touch. She felt a tightness below as Torrie kissed her. She shivered as Torrie stripped the clothes from her body then moved over her.

Diana helped Torrie out of her clothes and gasped with pleasure as Torrie's body covered her. Torrie's skin felt like warm silk.

Diana trembled as Torrie caressed her inner thighs. She heard the sound of her own voice calling Torrie's name as Torrie touched the wetness between her legs. She shuddered as Torrie sucked her inside and ran her tongue against the firmness of the pearl. She surrendered totally. Exalted, she lost all sense of time and space.

She felt like she was exploding into a thousand suns. Diana was part of them now, fire and light, heat and energy. Destruction and creation were hers. She pushed hard against the throbbing beat that consumed her.

Her body suddenly arched upward, engulfed by waves of ecstasy. Never before was love like this.

"Torrie!" she screamed. "Yes, Torrie, yes!"

They were one — one heart, one soul, one love.

Torrie's body covered hers as she floated in complete fulfillment. The glow from the sun painted Torrie's face with golden light.

"I love you," Diana said. She felt completely

relaxed. Then she thought of Torrie's round hips and wet, silken lips. "I want you, Torrie. Come over me so I can taste you."

Torrie kissed her, then knelt over her. She lowered herself to within inches of Diana's mouth.

"You're so beautiful." Diana fondled the silken lips that waited just above her.

"That feels so good," Torrie murmured.

Diana cradled Torrie's hips and pulled her downward. She caressed the firm, pink pearl, sucking it into her mouth, holding it firmly and stroking it with her tongue.

Torrie gasped with pleasure, as she pressed herself against Diana's mouth and fingers. Suddenly, Torrie screamed, her body convulsing in ecstasy. Again she shuddered, and called Diana's name, then fell beside her. Through slippery kisses, she said, "I love you. I love the way we taste."

Diana wrapped Torrie in her arms and pulled one of the beach towels over them. They drifted into sleep, fully satisfied, completely happy and in love.

The sound of seagulls and the touch of waves lapping at her ankles half-woke Diana from sleep. She moved closer to Torrie and hugged her. She wanted to re-enter sleep, to pursue Torrie across her dreams, to catch, hold, and caress her forever.

Wings grazed her ear as a seagull flew perilously close on his way to the picnic. The cold insistence of waves lapped at her fingertips. When the next wave arrived, its cold spray shocked her into wakefulness. She opened her eyes in time to see two seagulls fly away, carrying several crackers and the bright gold foil from the champagne bottle in their beaks.

"Good grief!" Diana shouted. "The tide's coming

in!" She shook Torrie and jumped to her feet, just in time to see the red and white Igloo ice chest, champagne and all, carried out to sea.

Torrie jumped up and rubbed the sleep from her eyes.

"The champagne is floating away!" Diana shouted. The ice chest was bobbing up and down between waves.

Stark naked, Torrie ran forward. "I'll get it," she called. She was knee deep in the water when she realized what was happening. "Good God! This water is freezing," Torrie shouted, and staggered on to the beach. "The champagne is beyond redemption." She stomped her feet on the sand. "My feet may also be beyond redemption."

As she threw a beach towel in Torrie's direction, Diana saw the first waves lapping at the red tablecloth. "Torrie, our picnic is about to set sail!" Diana laughed.

The two grabbed the tablecloth and dragged it up the beach. They almost had it, but then a large rock jutted beneath the cloth. The turkey was knocked off balance and it rolled down the beach, and into the water.

"Oh, no!" Diana cried. "There goes our dinner!"

Torrie dropped the tablecloth, sending the container of potato salad after the turkey. "I'll get it!" Torrie shouted. She lunged down the beach, making several futile grabs for the potato salad, and lost her balance, falling face-first into the incoming tide. Another wave brought the turkey close to her and she lunged for it.

"Torrie, are you all right?" Diana called.

Torrie stood up, a turkey leg clutched in her

hand, like a trophy, seawater dripping from her face and hair.

"Get out of the water. You'll get pneumonia!"

Torrie looked at herself. "Pneumonia? Diana, pneumonia would be an improvement!" She trudged up the beach and put her arm around Diana. "This towel is soaked," she said. "I'm not sure which is worse — being naked and cold, or covered and freezing."

"Neither has much in its favor," Diana said. "I suggest we let the rest of this follow the champagne. Let's get some clothes on, and fix omelets for dinner." She began to laugh. "This is unbelievable! No one would believe this in a hundred years."

"Don't worry, I don't plan to tell anyone."

Diana shook Torrie's hand. "Deal. I'll race you to the house. The last one there does the dishes!" Diana grabbed Torrie's arm. "Just one more thing. Happy Thanksgiving! It's one neither of us will ever forget." She kissed Torrie on the cheek. "All right. On the count of three. One, two, three . . ."

CHAPTER 32

"Torrie, be careful. You'll break its branches," Diana said. "Move a little to your left."

Torrie dutifully moved two steps to her left. There was a loud thud, followed by a snapping sound, followed by the sound of a small branch hitting the wooden porch floor.

"Oh, no!" Diana shouted. "It's broken." Diana dropped her end of the six-foot Norwegian Spruce they had purchased for their first Christmas.

"Maybe I should walk backwards and you should carry this end."

"It won't matter, Diana," Torrie said, amused. "The tree is too full to get through the door without crushing it a little bit."

"This isn't funny, Torrie," Diana said, eyeballing the tree then the doorway. "Maybe if you lift your end about thirty degrees and move a step to the right . . ."

"Diana!" Torrie exclaimed. "I told you back at the lot that the tree is wider than the door. The fact is if we're going to get the thing inside, we're going to knock a few needles off. Our other option is to set it up out here."

"Very funny," she said. "I'm not sure your parents would appreciate a decorated outdoor Christmas tree."

"Forget my parents," Torrie said. "It's our tree. I say we pick the thing up, head straight for the center of the doorway, run it into the house, and let the needles fall where they may."

Diana shrugged. "You're right. Let's do it. Pick up your end." She waited for Torrie to comply, then picked up the stump of the tree trunk. "Take one step to your right . . . That's it. Stop. You're exactly in the center of the doorway. Okay, I'll count to three. On three, we move like lightning."

"Like lightning!" Torrie laughed. "This thing is heavy. I'll move as fast as I can. If you step on a body on your way in, you'll know you ran me over."

"Your fate is in your feet, my dear!" Diana said. "Ready! One. Two. Three!"

They rammed the tree through the door. The sound of rustling branches and the smell of sap filled the air.

"Deo gratias!" Diana shouted from behind the tree.

"If that means we did it," Torrie said, "I second the motion."

"It means 'Thanks be to God,'" Diana said. "Let's get it in the stand."

"Hey, I didn't see God carrying Her end of the tree," Torrie said. "Let's give credit where credit is due."

"Your humility is overwhelming," Diana said as they slipped the tree into the stand.

Torrie grinned up at Diana. "There. The screws are all in place. You can let go." For a moment, they both watched Winston as he inspected the tree stand and sniffed at the branches. "It's beautiful even without lights and decorations. It will be stunning when we're finished."

Diana looked at the tree and then at Torrie. "I believe you're right. By the time your parents get here, our tree will be awesome!"

"The place looks really nice." Torrie's mother looked up at the stained glass window. "Very unusual," she said. "Very beautiful."

"May I get you something to drink, Victor? Coffee, tea, hot apple cider?" Diana asked. Her face was a little pale and her voice was slightly unsteady.

"Apple cider would be nice," Victor said. He laid several large packages on the end of the refectory table.

Elizabeth turned and looked at Diana. For a moment there was dead silence.

"Mother, would you like a cup of hot cider?" Torrie watched her mother and hoped the awkwardness of the moment would pass quickly.

"Yes. Cider sounds wonderful. But please don't go to too much trouble for us, Diane."

"Diana, Mother," Torrie said. "Not Diane." She was annoyed at her mother's all-too-familiar way of conveniently forgetting the name of a person she disliked or didn't really want to interact with.

"Of course," Elizabeth said. "Forgive me. I'm not very good with names."

"Don't give it a second thought," Diana said. "I'll get the cider. Please make yourselves comfortable."

When Diana left, Torrie was aware of a chill in the room.

"I'll put another log on the fire," she said. "Come sit down and talk to me."

Torrie gave her attention to the fireplace for a moment, added two logs and replaced the screen.

"So how have you been?" Victor asked.

Torrie relaxed into her favorite chair across from the sofa. "Are you asking as a physician, or as my father?"

"Both," he said. "Have the headaches increased in frequency or severity?"

Torrie wasn't sure she wanted to talk about her headaches. She'd rather this be a happy visit. "About the same," she lied.

"That's a good sign," he said, visibly relaxing. "That's good news."

"It certainly is," her mother chimed in. She sounded happy. "We'd like you and Diana to go on a

Caribbean cruise with us the first two weeks in February. The warm weather and relaxation would do you both good."

They've accepted her, Torrie thought. They've accepted us. She was relieved. "That sounds good. Are you sure you want us to go with you?"

"Your mother and I have done a lot of thinking, and a lot of talking," her father said. He glanced at his wife and then back to Torrie. "We both agree that if this woman . . ."

"Diana. Her name is Diana," Torrie said, determined to have them show some respect, if nothing else, for her and for their relationship.

"Excuse me," he said. "Diana. If Diana makes you happy, and if she's important to you — she obviously cares — about you, then she's important to us. We want to be included in your life."

At that moment, Diana returned, carrying a tray with four mugs. Torrie welcomed the reprieve; she hadn't expected this turn of events, especially from her father.

"That smells wonderful," her mother said, clearly grateful for the change of subject. "The aroma always reminds me of Christmas."

"I know what you mean," Diana said. "I have a lot of fond memories of Christmas and hot apple cider."

"Mom and Dad have invited us on a two-week Caribbean cruise in February," Torrie said to Diana.

"That sounds like fun." Diana smiled at Torrie's parents. "It's very kind of you to ask us. I'd love to go."

"Then it's settled," Victor said. "We'll make the reservations today."

185

"It sounds like such fun. Why don't you see if we can get reservations in January?" Elizabeth asked.

"That might be a problem, Mom. Diana and I are going to Chicago for a week in January."

"Whatever for? Chicago will be like a walk-in freezer in January," Elizabeth said. "Can't you change your plans?"

"I'm afraid not. We're committed and looking forward to the trip," Torrie said.

"That's no problem. We'll just stick with February," Victor said.

"Do you have relatives in Chicago, Diana?" Elizabeth asked.

"Sort of," Diana said. "They're like family."

Torrie hoped her mother would drop the subject. She definitely didn't want to lose the new-found acceptance they had offered, and she wasn't at all sure how her mother would respond to her speaking with, let alone visiting Aunt Susan.

"In deference to Torrie, couldn't you visit your friends in February?" Elizabeth asked.

Here we go, Torrie thought.

"Mom, we're going to visit Aunt Susan. She and Joyce were here last month."

Her mother's face turned ashen. "When did you start talking to Susan?"

"In October," Torrie said. "I think she'd really like to talk to you too. I know she misses the kind of relationship you two had when you were growing up."

Her mother looked shocked and hurt. "Whatever made you contact her, Torrie? You knew my feelings concerning Susan."

"I wanted to meet her, Mom. I wanted to know

her side of the story." Torrie watched her mother closely. "I felt I might understand my own history better if I could talk to her." She paused. "I felt pretty sure she'd understand where I was coming from, and I needed that kind of understanding."

"Didn't you think your father and I understood you?"

"Mom, you were having your own problems accepting things. I'm not judging you for that. I understand how difficult this whole situation must be for you and Dad." She glanced at Diana for assurance, then continued. "You have no idea how happy it made us to hear you were coming here today. You're my parents and I love you very much. I really appreciate your acceptance. Your being here today tells me that we have it. I think we both know what you must have gone through to reach this point. Diana's parents haven't spoken to her since she told them about us. I can imagine how Aunt Susan must have felt when she was disowned by the family. That's partly why I called her . . . She's a wonderful person, Mom. She reminds me a lot of you. You look so much alike, anyone would know you were related."

"I'm sure she didn't have much good to say about me." Her mother's eyes spoke questions unasked.

"She had a lot of good things to say about you. Including telling me how much you loved me. She encouraged me to talk to you and work out any misunderstandings between us."

"She did?" Elizabeth said. Her tone was one of surprise and relief.

"Yes, she did," Torrie said. Tears had begun to form in her mother's eyes. "I wish you'd call her,

Mom. She really does miss you." She watched as her mother dabbed at her tears with a tissue. "Joyce Branson has been her companion for the last twenty years. She teaches English literature. She's heard so many stories from Aunt Susan about when you two were growing up that she feels she knows you. I think the two of you would like each other a lot."

"Susan always was crazy about reading." Her mother smiled. "For someone who wanted to be a physician, she had an inordinate love of literature and poetry."

"She still does," Torrie said. "I hope you'll consider calling her. You two have a lot to catch up on."

"I'll give it serious consideration." Elizabeth said, "I do miss her at times." It was a big admission for her mother to make, Torrie knew, and she was sure her mother had dealt all she could with the subject of Susan for the moment.

Her mother looked at her watch. "I'm afraid we need to be going if we're going to get to John and Edna's tonight."

"Are you sure you can't stay?" Torrie asked. "We have plenty of room and you can share Christmas brunch with us and Mark Mason. He asked me to invite you if you decided to spend the night. How about it? We'd love to have you."

"That's nice of you and Doctor Mason," Elizabeth said, "but we really can't." She stood up. "We'll drop by again on our way back the day after New Year's. All right?"

"We'll look forward to it," Torrie said. "You'll be our first company for the new year."

* * * * *

It was two o'clock when they returned home the next afternoon from Mark Mason's Christmas brunch.

"I'll build a fire if you'll bring us a cup of hot cider," Torrie said, giving Diana a kiss.

"Want something to eat? A piece of pie or fruitcake?" Diana asked.

"No, thanks. I'm stuffed from brunch," Torrie said.

"Two ciders coming up," Diana said, starting for the kitchen.

"Hurry back so we can open our presents." Torrie slapped her playfully on the backside.

Diana was right about the tree, Torrie thought as she laid the fire. The lights and decorations had indeed turned the room into an "awesome spectacle." She smiled to herself and glanced at the packages stacked beneath the tree. It had been a hard fight for her not to give Diana one of her presents ahead of time. Now she was glad Diana had insisted on waiting until Christmas to open it. Diana had teased her unmercifully in those weeks before Christmas calling her "Christmas Pushover."

"I'll just be a few minutes," Diana called from the kitchen.

"Take your time. I'm not going anywhere," Torrie called back, staring up at the stained glass window. It seemed to get more beautiful every time she looked at it — the wings of the dove in flight, the olive branch held firmly in its beak. Life goes on, she thought, and will go on.

She looked out the plate glass window below.

There wasn't a snow cloud in sight. She never could get used to Christmases with temperatures near sixty degrees. She turned the radio on. The sound of "It Came Upon a Midnight Clear" filled the room.

"Oh, good." Diana's voice preceded her into the room. "You've found some Christmas carols."

Torrie laughed. "Since they're on every station, there's no trick to finding them."

Diana handed Torrie a mug of cider and squeezed in beside her. She clicked her mug against Torrie's. "To us, and to Christmas!"

They sat and watched the fire for a while, then Torrie said, "You stay there. It's time to open presents. Winston and I have waited long enough to find out what Santa has left us." Winston barked and followed Torrie to the tree. "I guess we can open yours first, Winston."

"Sounds fair to me," Diana said. "Bring me the one with the reindeer paper, and the one with the snowmen."

Torrie placed six presents on the coffee table in front of Diana. She held up a long L-shaped package covered with candy canes and teddy bears. "This is yours, Winston." She placed it on the floor and let Winston inspect it. "Okay, boy. Let me open it for you." Winston danced around in a circle as Torrie unwrapped the package and held up a long, fishnet stocking filled with rawhide bones, hard rubber toys, a small ball and a slipper. "It looks as if Santa Dog has been pretty good to you," Torrie said.

Winston picked up one toy and then another, completely engrossed.

"Well, he looks happy," Torrie said. "We're next."

She handed Diana a red envelope. "Open this one first."

Diana opened the envelope and read the card inside. "Good for one waterproof, ten-pound turkey, and one beach picnic on the day of your choice." Diana laughed. "The way the weather has been going, we can probably use this in a week or two." She pointed to the larger package with reindeer. "You open that one next."

Torrie loved opening presents almost as much as she liked giving them. Feeling like a five-year-old, she tore into the packages.

"Read the card first," Diana said.

Torrie took the card from the last piece of red tissue paper, read aloud, "To replace the one that got away!" She ripped through the rest of the wrappings. "Just what I needed." She held up a red and white Igloo ice chest and a bottle of champagne. "It looks as if we're ready for that picnic." She handed Diana a small, dark blue box.

"Oh, Torrie!" Diana exclaimed. "It's beautiful!" The gold pendant Torrie had specially made was cut in the shape of a dove in flight. In its beak was a small gold olive branch.

"It's the dove from our window!" Diana said. Her voice was almost a whisper. She leaned forward and kissed her.

"Turn it over," Torrie said. "You haven't read the inscription."

" 'Forever.' " Diana looked up. "It's perfect. It's the first and only piece of jewelry I own. My first ever perfect Christmas present." She held it up against her chest. "Help me put it on."

Torrie fastened the clasp on the gold chain, turned Diana around and said, "You were made for each other."

"Like us," Diana said. She pointed to another box. "Now it's your turn. Open that one next."

Torrie ripped through the bright Christmas paper. From a small gray jewelry box she removed one of two hammered gold bands and slipped it on the third finger of her left hand. "It's a perfect fit," Torrie said, surprised.

"It should be. I went to great lengths to get your ring size without letting you guess what I was up to."

"You surprised me completely," Torrie said. She lifted the other band from the box. "And I would guess that this one fits you perfectly."

"It does," Diana said. "But read the inscription first. The inscription in each ring is identical."

Torrie removed her band and read, " 'Stay, Thou Art So Fair!' "

Torrie felt stunned. She remembered the scene from Goethe's *Faust*. Faust had sold his soul to the Devil on the condition that the Devil could collect, if and only when Faust had found such perfect happiness that he would have all time stand still, and the moment last forever. Had Diana found that moment with her? Did she value her time with Torrie more than all the years that had passed, and all the years that might be in the future?

To be so loved, Torrie thought, to be so undeniably valued by the woman who meant more to her than life itself. To look Eternity in the face, she thought, was to *know* that if she had every moment Eternity held, she could not possess more than she had at that very moment. She and Diana had created the eternal moment and would live in its love together, forever. Not even God could alter that fact!

Torrie was suddenly aware of the heat of Diana's body and the clean scent of her skin. The crackling and popping of the fire surrounded them; the dark depths of Diana's eyes compelled her to enter; and the taste of Diana's kiss filled her mouth and her memory.

In one movement, Torrie reached for her, slipped the hammered gold band on the third finger of her left hand, and kissed the center of her palm.

Intoxicated, Torrie yielded completely as Diana slipped the matching band on the third finger of Torrie's left hand.

Torrie kissed her softly, then began undressing her. Firelight moved over Diana's skin and Torrie traced its moving outline first with her fingers, and then with her mouth. Diana responded, removing Torrie's clothes and caressing her breasts and nipples. Christmas music played in the background as Torrie gathered Diana to herself and lay down with her before the blazing fire. With deliberate slowness, she traced the curves of Diana's breasts and squeezed each nipple gently between her fingers.

Diana's legs opened willingly as Torrie kissed her way upward along the silk of her inner thighs and swallowed the pink-red mysteries that lay between. Like notes falling into place in a concerto, Torrie's strokes called forth new music, with new and deeper rhythms. She reached up, caressing Diana's breasts, then found her way down Diana's body and inward to the burning well. Her fingers glided in, and the inner walls closed around her.

Diana's moans and cries doubled Torrie's excitement, but suddenly, Diana was pulling her upward away from the soft mysteries and the pearl. Before Torrie could utter a word, Diana was gliding in the warm wetness of their love, was kissing, taking Torrie's tongue deep into her mouth.

Diana held Torrie's face between her hands and looked directly into her eyes. "I want you at the same time."

They kissed again, and without a word Torrie covered Diana's body so that each had perfect access to the other. She shuddered as she felt Diana's tongue move along the soft inner lips between her thighs. Like an incoming tide, pleasure swept over her.

Torrie buried her head between Diana's thighs and sucked the swollen pearl into her mouth. She held it against the firmness of her teeth as her head moved back and forth. She gasped as she felt herself sucked into Diana's mouth and felt her own actions repeated.

Balanced on the razor's edge of ecstasy, Torrie heard her own cries echoed by Diana's. The vibration of the sound enhanced her pleasure and she pressed harder and stroked faster against Diana's swollen pearl. Diana mirrored Torrie's actions, and Torrie shuddered as wave after wave of exquisite pleasure swept her deeper into the heart of union with Diana.

Diana shuddered beneath her as she called Torrie's name.

Suddenly she and Diana were holding each other, exchanging tender kisses, speaking their love.

Torrie kissed Diana's ear and brushed her lips lightly against it. She spoke in barely a whisper.

"Diana, I love you more than I can possibly tell you. I love you more than I have ever loved anyone or anything in my life." She traced Diana's face with her fingers, then turned her toward her. "I can't think of a more fitting inscription than the one engraved in our rings." Torrie's love overflowed into silent tears. "I feel exactly as Faust must have when he said, 'Stay, thou art so fair.' Sometimes it frightens me to think that I might have lived a millennium and never found that moment."

Diana embraced her and kissed her softly on the mouth.

"You've given me that moment, Diana," Torrie said. "You've given that rarest of gifts to me in just a few short months. If I had the power, I would stop time and spend eternity as we are now. I know, really and truly know, that I could not possibly be happier than I am right now. You have given me more happiness, more closeness, than most people even dream of having."

Diana wiped the tears from Torrie's face and kissed her.

"I'm not looking forward to dying, Diana, but for the first time in my life I know what it means to really live. I know that it has nothing to do with length of days, or the number of candles on the last birthday cake. I know now that the essence of living is loving and being loved. And that the essence of loving is commitment. Commitment given, and commitment received. That, in that commitment two people create a new and spiritual reality — a spiritual being that is born of love." She smiled.

"We've created that being, Diana, and neither time nor death can diminish it. What we are together

195

can never die." Torrie held Diana's face between her hands. "If we had a thousand years together, I could not possibly love you more than I do at this very moment."

Diana kissed her and held her closer to herself. "You asked me once why I would choose to give my love to God rather than to a flesh-and-blood person. At the time, I didn't quite understand the question, let alone what the answer might be." She looked into Torrie's eyes. "I know now that you've taught me more about love than I learned in all my years as a nun. Not that I love God less, but that I love you more. I wouldn't trade the way I feel for a thousand years of guaranteed security." She smiled and kissed Torrie gently. "I love you, Torrie Lassiter. Not even God can change that."

CHAPTER 33

The music from "Ice Castles" floated onto the deck and upward into the clear night sky.

"I hope Mark wasn't too disappointed about us not going down there tonight," Torrie said.

"He seemed to understand that we're both tired and need some time to ourselves," Diana said. "I told him we'd stop by tomorrow." Diana brushed her fingertips over Torrie's forehead as she cradled Torrie's head in her lap. "I can't think of a better way to spend Christmas night."

"I think all the excitement has tired Winston out," Torrie said, glancing at Winston. He was lying on her legs, curled up and sound asleep. "He's probably dreaming of next Christmas. This one is almost over. It must be close to midnight."

"Well, the Christmas sky will last until morning no matter what the clocks say." Diana stroked Torrie's face. "Is your head any better? The medication should be taking effect by now."

"It's much better," Torrie said. "Just a dull ache." There's no need to tell her how bad the pain really is, Torrie thought. It would only frighten her and ruin the rest of the evening. If I can just keep still, it isn't quite so bad. Movement seemed to make it worse. "As long as I can lie here like this, I have no complaints. I get to see you and the sky all at the same time. It's a perfect view."

Diana hugged Torrie closer. "I love holding you. I could stay like this all night. Just looking at you makes me feel warm inside."

"I'm glad you're happy," Torrie said. She looked up at Diana's face. The moonlight's reflection on Diana's skin had decreased considerably. She looked at the stars. They too seemed much dimmer than they had been only moments before. Torrie's heart raced as she realized what was happening. She looked in the direction of the halogen light near the doorway to their bedroom. She could barely see its outline — a thin, fading bluish line against a backdrop of darkness. Her heart began to pound wildly. She rested her head in Diana's lap and fought to maintain her composure. *I'm dying,* her words echoed in her mind. "Are you all right?" Diana asked. "You look pale all of a sudden." She reached for Torrie's pulse.

"Your pulse is going as if you've just run the Boston Marathon."

Don't let her know, Torrie thought. There's nothing she can do. We've said our good-byes. We both know how much we love each other. Don't upset her. Make the most of the time that's left.

Torrie exerted a conscious effort to slow her heart rate. "I was thinking of our picnic on Thanksgiving Day. That was enough to get my heart racing again," Torrie said in a calm voice. She glanced up. She could see Diana's eyes, her smile, but they were fading quickly, as if some unseen hand were slowly turning a dimmer switch to the off position.

"The music is beautiful," Diana said as the sounds of "How Do You Keep the Music Playing" floated toward them. "Would you like to dance?"

Torrie's heart was thudding against her chest. "I'd rather just stay here, if it's all right with you." Torrie strained against the veil of darkness that was slowly closing over her. She could barely see the outline of Diana's face. Moonlight bathed Diana's eyes and mouth in silver, silhouetting them in the encroaching darkness. She's so beautiful, Torrie thought, so very beautiful. "Give me your hand, Diana," she said. "I want to feel your skin next to mine."

Diana placed her hand in Torrie's, lacing her fingers through Torrie's, pressing her palm against Torrie's palm. Torrie gripped Diana's hand in response. Torrie felt herself melt into Diana's skin; felt her boundaries falling away; felt herself merging with Diana.

"I love the way your skin feels against mine," Diana said. "I hardly know where I stop and you begin."

"I think we've loved each other to the point where we've truly become part of each other, truly become a new being together." Torrie fought the urge to squeeze Diana's hand tighter. She opened her eyes wider to let in more light, to see Diana's face one last time. Diana's smile flashed visible for a moment, and was gone. Torrie drew Diana's hand to her lips and kissed the back of Diana's fingers.

Dear God, Torrie thought, *please take care of her when I'm gone. And please, if there is any way to let her know I'm waiting for her — let me find that way.* Torrie was heartbroken, not at her own death, but at the thought of leaving Diana.

"You're awfully quiet," Diana said. "Where are you, and what are you thinking about?"

"I'm right here with you," Torrie said. "And I was wondering how many times you and I had been lovers in the past, and how many times we'll be lovers again in the future."

Diana laughed, and the sound was like music to Torrie. "I don't ever intend to let you get away from me, Torrie Lassiter. I know that you and I will recognize each other no matter what bodies we're in." Torrie felt Diana's lips against her mouth. "Accept it, Doc, you're never going to be free of me."

Torrie smiled. "You have no idea how comforting I find that thought. I love you, Diana."

"I'm glad," Diana said. "I'd hate to be the only person on this deck who is madly in love."

"Rest assured, my darling, you are not alone," Torrie said. "I will love you forever."

Torrie felt suddenly lighter and very sleepy. She squeezed Diana's hand and allowed herself to drift.

They sat in silence for almost twenty minutes. Diana watched the night sky, drinking in its beauty. Suddenly there was a shift in the wind, and for a moment a cloud covered the face of the moon.

"The wind is rising," she said. "Are you cold, Torrie?" Before Torrie had time to answer, Diana's attention was captured by the sky. "Torrie! Look up quick! There's a shooting star! The brightest one I've ever seen . . . it's beautiful! Do you see it?"

Winston cried out in his sleep as if he were having a bad dream.

Diana was suddenly aware that Torrie hadn't moved. The music of "I'll Be Seeing You" was playing quietly.

Diana looked down. Torrie's face was peaceful and relaxed. Suddenly Diana's heart started pounding. Something was wrong. She's not breathing, Diana thought. She put her fingers against Torrie's neck, feeling for the pulse of the carotid artery. Nothing!

"No, Torrie!" she cried, tears streaming down her face. "Not yet! They promised us more time together." She bent forward and hugged Torrie's lifeless body. "It's too soon, Torrie, much too soon." Diana held her and rocked back and forth as if comforting a child. "What will I do without you? What will I do?"

* * * * *

201

Time passed, and Diana finally stood up, laid Torrie's head gently on the swing, and went into the living room. She dialed Mark Mason's number, and when he answered, said simply: "Mark, Torrie is gone. Could you come up here for a while?"

She replaced the receiver and glanced up at the stained glass window. She felt her heart skip as she realized the window was broken, and the dove was gone. She scanned the floor. A large branch was lying on the back of the sofa, and there was a small shiny object on the cushion of Torrie's chair.

Diana walked to the chair and picked the object up. It was a piece of the stained glass window, an almost perfect circle, and in its center was the dove in flight, the olive branch still held firmly in its beak. She held the stained-glass dove in her palm and looked at the pendant around her neck. The doves were almost identical. She turned the pendant over and read the inscription aloud: "Forever." She looked up at the stained glass window. "Yes, my love, I hear you. I love you, Torrie. I will love you forever!"

A few of the publications of
THE NAIAD PRESS, INC.
P.O. Box 10543 • Tallahassee, Florida 32302
Phone (904) 539-5965
Toll-Free Order Number: 1-800-533-1973
Mail orders welcome. Please include 15% postage.

FOREVER by Evelyn Kennedy. 224 pp. Passionate romance — love overcoming all obstacles. ISBN 1-56280-094-9 $10.95

WHISPERS by Kris Bruyer. 224 pp. Romantic ghost story ISBN 1-56280-082-5 10.95

NIGHT SONGS by Penny Mickelbury. 224 pp. A Gianna Maglione Mystery. Second in a series. ISBN 1-56280-097-3 10.95

GETTING TO THE POINT by Teresa Stores. 256 pp. Classic southern Lesbian novel. ISBN 1-56280-100-7 10.95

PAINTED MOON by Karin Kallmaker. 224 pp. Delicious Kallmaker romance. ISBN 1-56280-075-2 9.95

THE MYSTERIOUS NAIAD edited by Katherine V. Forrest & Barbara Grier. 320 pp. Love stories by Naiad Press authors. ISBN 1-56280-074-4 14.95

DAUGHTERS OF A CORAL DAWN by Katherine V. Forrest. 240 pp. Tenth Anniversay Edition. ISBN 1-56280-104-X 10.95

BODY GUARD by Claire McNab. 208 pp. A Carol Ashton Mystery. 6th in a series. ISBN 1-56280-073-6 9.95

CACTUS LOVE by Lee Lynch. 192 pp. Stories by the beloved storyteller. ISBN 1-56280-071-X 9.95

SECOND GUESS by Rose Beecham. 216 pp. An Amanda Valentine Mystery. 2nd in a series. ISBN 1-56280-069-8 9.95

THE SURE THING by Melissa Hartman. 208 pp. L.A. earthquake romance. ISBN 1-56280-078-7 9.95

A RAGE OF MAIDENS by Lauren Wright Douglas. 240 pp. A Caitlin Reece Mystery. 6th in a series. ISBN 1-56280-068-X 9.95

TRIPLE EXPOSURE by Jackie Calhoun. 224 pp. Romantic drama involving many characters. ISBN 1-56280-067-1 9.95

UP, UP AND AWAY by Catherine Ennis. 192 pp. Delightful romance. ISBN 1-56280-065-5 9.95

PERSONAL ADS by Robbi Sommers. 176 pp. Sizzling short stories. ISBN 1-56280-059-0 9.95

FLASHPOINT by Katherine V. Forrest. 256 pp. Lesbian
blockbuster! ISBN 1-56280-043-4 22.95

CROSSWORDS by Penny Sumner. 256 pp. 2nd Victoria Cross
Mystery. ISBN 1-56280-064-7 9.95

SWEET CHERRY WINE by Carol Schmidt. 224 pp. A novel of
suspense. ISBN 1-56280-063-9 9.95

CERTAIN SMILES by Dorothy Tell. 160 pp. Erotic short stories.
ISBN 1-56280-066-3 9.95

EDITED OUT by Lisa Haddock. 224 pp. 1st Carmen Ramirez
Mystery. ISBN 1-56280-077-9 9.95

WEDNESDAY NIGHTS by Camarin Grae. 288 pp. Sexy
adventure. ISBN 1-56280-060-4 10.95

SMOKEY O by Celia Cohen. 176 pp. Relationships on the
playing field. ISBN 1-56280-057-4 9.95

KATHLEEN O'DONALD by Penny Hayes. 256 pp. Rose and
Kathleen find each other and employment in 1909 NYC.
ISBN 1-56280-070-1 9.95

STAYING HOME by Elisabeth Nonas. 256 pp. Molly and Alix
want a baby . . . or do they? ISBN 1-56280-076-0 10.95

TRUE LOVE by Jennifer Fulton. 240 pp. Six lesbians searching
for love in all the "right" places. ISBN 1-56280-035-3 9.95

GARDENIAS WHERE THERE ARE NONE by Molleen Zanger.
176 pp. Why is Melanie inextricably drawn to the old house?
ISBN 1-56280-056-6 9.95

KEEPING SECRETS by Penny Mickelbury. 208 pp. A Gianna
Maglione Mystery. First in a series. ISBN 1-56280-052-3 9.95

THE ROMANTIC NAIAD edited by Katherine V. Forrest &
Barbara Grier. 336 pp. Love stories by Naiad Press authors.
ISBN 1-56280-054-X 14.95

UNDER MY SKIN by Jaye Maiman. 336 pp. A Robin Miller
mystery. 3rd in a series. ISBN 1-56280-049-3. 10.95

STAY TOONED by Rhonda Dicksion. 144 pp. Cartoons — 1st
collection since *Lesbian Survival Manual.* ISBN 1-56280-045-0 9.95

CAR POOL by Karin Kallmaker. 272pp. Lesbians on wheels
and then some! ISBN 1-56280-048-5 9.95

NOT TELLING MOTHER: STORIES FROM A LIFE by Diane
Salvatore. 176 pp. Her 3rd novel. ISBN 1-56280-044-2 9.95

GOBLIN MARKET by Lauren Wright Douglas. 240pp. A Caitlin
Reece Mystery. 5th in a series. ISBN 1-56280-047-7 10.95

LONG GOODBYES by Nikki Baker. 256 pp. A Virginia Kelly
mystery. 3rd in a series. ISBN 1-56280-042-6 9.95

FRIENDS AND LOVERS by Jackie Calhoun. 224 pp. Mid-western
Lesbian lives and loves.   ISBN 1-56280-041-8   10.95

THE CAT CAME BACK by Hilary Mullins. 208 pp. Highly
praised Lesbian novel.   ISBN 1-56280-040-X   9.95

BEHIND CLOSED DOORS by Robbi Sommers. 192 pp. Hot,
erotic short stories.   ISBN 1-56280-039-6   9.95

CLAIRE OF THE MOON by Nicole Conn. 192 pp. See the
movie — read the book!   ISBN 1-56280-038-8   10.95

SILENT HEART by Claire McNab. 192 pp. Exotic Lesbian
romance.   ISBN 1-56280-036-1   10.95

HAPPY ENDINGS by Kate Brandt. 272 pp. Intimate conversations
with Lesbian authors.   ISBN 1-56280-050-7   10.95

THE SPY IN QUESTION by Amanda Kyle Williams. 256 pp.
4th Madison McGuire.   ISBN 1-56280-037-X   9.95

SAVING GRACE by Jennifer Fulton. 240 pp. Adventure and
romantic entanglement.   ISBN 1-56280-051-5   9.95

THE YEAR SEVEN by Molleen Zanger. 208 pp. Women surviving
in a new world.   ISBN 1-56280-034-5   9.95

CURIOUS WINE by Katherine V. Forrest. 176 pp. Tenth Anniver-
sary Edition. The most popular contemporary Lesbian love story.
                                              ISBN 1-56280-053-1   10.95
          Audio Book (2 cassettes)   ISBN 1-56280-105-8   16.95

CHAUTAUQUA by Catherine Ennis. 192 pp. Exciting, romantic
adventure.   ISBN 1-56280-032-9   9.95

A PROPER BURIAL by Pat Welch. 192 pp. A Helen Black
mystery. 3rd in a series.   ISBN 1-56280-033-7   9.95

SILVERLAKE HEAT: A Novel of Suspense by Carol Schmidt.
240 pp. Rhonda is as hot as Laney's dreams.   ISBN 1-56280-031-0   9.95

LOVE, ZENA BETH by Diane Salvatore. 224 pp. The most talked
about lesbian novel of the nineties!   ISBN 1-56280-030-2   10.95

A DOORYARD FULL OF FLOWERS by Isabel Miller. 160 pp.
Stories incl. 2 sequels to *Patience and Sarah.* ISBN 1-56280-029-9   9.95

MURDER BY TRADITION by Katherine V. Forrest. 288 pp. A
Kate Delafield Mystery. 4th in a series.   ISBN 1-56280-002-7   9.95

THE EROTIC NAIAD edited by Katherine V. Forrest & Barbara
Grier. 224 pp. Love stories by Naiad Press authors.
                                              ISBN 1-56280-026-4   13.95

DEAD CERTAIN by Claire McNab. 224 pp. A Carol Ashton
mystery. 5th in a series.   ISBN 1-56280-027-2   9.95

CRAZY FOR LOVING by Jaye Maiman. 320 pp. A Robin Miller
mystery. 2nd in a series.   ISBN 1-56280-025-6   9.95

STONEHURST by Barbara Johnson. 176 pp. Passionate regency
romance. ISBN 1-56280-024-8 9.95

INTRODUCING AMANDA VALENTINE by Rose Beecham.
256 pp. An Amanda Valentine Mystery. First in a series.
ISBN 1-56280-021-3 9.95

UNCERTAIN COMPANIONS by Robbi Sommers. 204 pp.
Steamy, erotic novel. ISBN 1-56280-017-5 9.95

A TIGER'S HEART by Lauren W. Douglas. 240 pp. A Caitlin
Reece mystery. 4th in a series. ISBN 1-56280-018-3 9.95

PAPERBACK ROMANCE by Karin Kallmaker. 256 pp. A
delicious romance. ISBN 1-56280-019-1 9.95

MORTON RIVER VALLEY by Lee Lynch. 304 pp. Lee Lynch
at her best! ISBN 1-56280-016-7 9.95

THE LAVENDER HOUSE MURDER by Nikki Baker. 224 pp.
A Virginia Kelly Mystery. 2nd in a series. ISBN 1-56280-012-4 9.95

PASSION BAY by Jennifer Fulton. 224 pp. Passionate romance,
virgin beaches, tropical skies. ISBN 1-56280-028-0 10.95

STICKS AND STONES by Jackie Calhoun. 208 pp. Contemporary
lesbian lives and loves. ISBN 1-56280-020-5 9.95
Audio Book (2 cassettes) ISBN 1-56280-106-6 16.95

DELIA IRONFOOT by Jeane Harris. 192 pp. Adventure for Delia
and Beth in the Utah mountains. ISBN 1-56280-014-0 9.95

UNDER THE SOUTHERN CROSS by Claire McNab. 192 pp.
Romantic nights Down Under. ISBN 1-56280-011-6 9.95

GRASSY FLATS by Penny Hayes. 256 pp. Lesbian romance in
the '30s. ISBN 1-56280-010-8 9.95

A SINGULAR SPY by Amanda K. Williams. 192 pp. 3rd
Madison McGuire. ISBN 1-56280-008-6 8.95

THE END OF APRIL by Penny Sumner. 240 pp. A Victoria
Cross mystery. First in a series. ISBN 1-56280-007-8 8.95

HOUSTON TOWN by Deborah Powell. 208 pp. A Hollis
Carpenter mystery. ISBN 1-56280-006-X 8.95

KISS AND TELL by Robbi Sommers. 192 pp. Scorching stories
by the author of *Pleasures*. ISBN 1-56280-005-1 10.95

STILL WATERS by Pat Welch. 208 pp. A Helen Black mystery.
2nd in a series. ISBN 0-941483-97-5 9.95

TO LOVE AGAIN by Evelyn Kennedy. 208 pp. Wildly romantic
love story. ISBN 0-941483-85-1 9.95

IN THE GAME by Nikki Baker. 192 pp. A Virginia Kelly
mystery. First in a series. ISBN 1-56280-004-3 9.95

AVALON by Mary Jane Jones. 256 pp. A Lesbian Arthurian
romance. ISBN 0-941483-96-7 9.95

STRANDED by Camarin Grae. 320 pp. Entertaining, riveting
adventure. ISBN 0-941483-99-1   9.95

THE DAUGHTERS OF ARTEMIS by Lauren Wright Douglas.
240 pp. A Caitlin Reece mystery. 3rd in a series.
ISBN 0-941483-95-9   9.95

CLEARWATER by Catherine Ennis. 176 pp. Romantic secrets
of a small Louisiana town. ISBN 0-941483-65-7   8.95

THE HALLELUJAH MURDERS by Dorothy Tell. 176 pp. A
Poppy Dillworth mystery. 2nd in a series. ISBN 0-941483-88-6   8.95

SECOND CHANCE by Jackie Calhoun. 256 pp. Contemporary
Lesbian lives and loves. ISBN 0-941483-93-2   9.95

BENEDICTION by Diane Salvatore. 272 pp. Striking, contemporary romantic novel. ISBN 0-941483-90-8   9.95

BLACK IRIS by Jeane Harris. 192 pp. Caroline's hidden past . . .
ISBN 0-941483-68-1   8.95

TOUCHWOOD by Karin Kallmaker. 240 pp. Loving, May/
December romance. ISBN 0-941483-76-2   9.95

COP OUT by Claire McNab. 208 pp. A Carol Ashton mystery.
4th in a series. ISBN 0-941483-84-3   9.95

THE BEVERLY MALIBU by Katherine V. Forrest. 288 pp. A
Kate Delafield Mystery. 3rd in a series. ISBN 0-941483-48-7   10.95

THAT OLD STUDEBAKER by Lee Lynch. 272 pp. Andy's affair
with Regina and her attachment to her beloved car.
ISBN 0-941483-82-7   9.95

PASSION'S LEGACY by Lori Paige. 224 pp. Sarah is swept into
the arms of Augusta Pym in this delightful historical romance.
ISBN 0-941483-81-9   8.95

THE PROVIDENCE FILE by Amanda Kyle Williams. 256 pp.
Second Madison McGuire ISBN 0-941483-92-4   8.95

I LEFT MY HEART by Jaye Maiman. 320 pp. A Robin Miller
Mystery. First in a series. ISBN 0-941483-72-X   9.95

THE PRICE OF SALT by Patricia Highsmith (writing as Claire
Morgan). 288 pp. Classic lesbian novel, first issued in 1952 . . .
acknowledged by its author under her own, very famous, name.
ISBN 1-56280-003-5   9.95

SIDE BY SIDE by Isabel Miller. 256 pp. From beloved author of
Patience and Sarah. ISBN 0-941483-77-0   9.95

STAYING POWER: LONG TERM LESBIAN COUPLES by
Susan E. Johnson. 352 pp. Joys of coupledom. ISBN 0-941-483-75-4   14.95

SLICK by Camarin Grae. 304 pp. Exotic, erotic adventure.
ISBN 0-941483-74-6   9.95

NINTH LIFE by Lauren Wright Douglas. 256 pp. A Caitlin Reece
mystery. 2nd in a series. ISBN 0-941483-50-9   8.95

PLAYERS by Robbi Sommers. 192 pp. Sizzling, erotic novel.
ISBN 0-941483-73-8   9.95

MURDER AT RED ROOK RANCH by Dorothy Tell. 224 pp.
A Poppy Dillworth mystery. 1st in a series.   ISBN 0-941483-80-0   8.95

LESBIAN SURVIVAL MANUAL by Rhonda Dicksion. 112 pp.
Cartoons!   ISBN 0-941483-71-1   8.95

A ROOM FULL OF WOMEN by Elisabeth Nonas. 256 pp.
Contemporary Lesbian lives.   ISBN 0-941483-69-X   9.95

THEME FOR DIVERSE INSTRUMENTS by Jane Rule. 208 pp.
Powerful romantic lesbian stories.   ISBN 0-941483-63-0   8.95

CLUB 12 by Amanda Kyle Williams. 288 pp. Espionage thriller
featuring a lesbian agent!   ISBN 0-941483-64-9   8.95

DEATH DOWN UNDER by Claire McNab. 240 pp. A Carol
Ashton mystery. 3rd in a series.   ISBN 0-941483-39-8   9.95

MONTANA FEATHERS by Penny Hayes. 256 pp. Vivian and
Elizabeth find love in frontier Montana.   ISBN 0-941483-61-4   8.95

LIFESTYLES by Jackie Calhoun. 224 pp. Contemporary Lesbian
lives and loves.   ISBN 0-941483-57-6   9.95

WILDERNESS TREK by Dorothy Tell. 192 pp. Six women on
vacation learning ''new'' skills.   ISBN 0-941483-60-6   8.95

MURDER BY THE BOOK by Pat Welch. 256 pp. A Helen Black
Mystery. First in a series.   ISBN 0-941483-59-2   9.95

THERE'S SOMETHING I'VE BEEN MEANING TO TELL YOU
Ed. by Loralee MacPike. 288 pp. Gay men and lesbians coming out
to their children.   ISBN 0-941483-44-4   9.95

LIFTING BELLY by Gertrude Stein. Ed. by Rebecca Mark. 104 pp.
Erotic poetry.   ISBN 0-941483-51-7   8.95

AFTER THE FIRE by Jane Rule. 256 pp. Warm, human novel by
this incomparable author.   ISBN 0-941483-45-2   8.95

THREE WOMEN by March Hastings. 232 pp. Golden oldie. A
triangle among wealthy sophisticates.   ISBN 0-941483-43-6   8.95

PLEASURES by Robbi Sommers. 204 pp. Unprecedented
eroticism.   ISBN 0-941483-49-5   8.95

EDGEWISE by Camarin Grae. 372 pp. Spellbinding
adventure.   ISBN 0-941483-19-3   9.95

FATAL REUNION by Claire McNab. 224 pp. A Carol Ashton
mystery. 2nd in a series.   ISBN 0-941483-40-1   8.95

IN EVERY PORT by Karin Kallmaker. 228 pp. Jessica's sexy,
adventuresome travels.   ISBN 0-941483-37-7   9.95

OF LOVE AND GLORY by Evelyn Kennedy. 192 pp. Exciting
WWII romance.   ISBN 0-941483-32-0   8.95

CLICKING STONES by Nancy Tyler Glenn. 288 pp. Love
transcending time. ISBN 0-941483-31-2   9.95

SOUTH OF THE LINE by Catherine Ennis. 216 pp. Civil War
adventure. ISBN 0-941483-29-0   8.95

WOMAN PLUS WOMAN by Dolores Klaich. 300 pp. Supurb
Lesbian overview. ISBN 0-941483-28-2   9.95

THE FINER GRAIN by Denise Ohio. 216 pp. Brilliant young
college lesbian novel. ISBN 0-941483-11-8   8.95

OCTOBER OBSESSION by Meredith More. Josie's rich, secret
Lesbian life. ISBN 0-941483-18-5   8.95

BEFORE STONEWALL: THE MAKING OF A GAY AND
LESBIAN COMMUNITY by Andrea Weiss & Greta Schiller.
96 pp., 25 illus. ISBN 0-941483-20-7   7.95

OSTEN'S BAY by Zenobia N. Vole. 204 pp. Sizzling adventure
romance set on Bonaire. ISBN 0-941483-15-0   8.95

LESSONS IN MURDER by Claire McNab. 216 pp. A Carol
Ashton mystery. First in a series. ISBN 0-941483-14-2   9.95

YELLOWTHROAT by Penny Hayes. 240 pp. Margarita, bandit,
kidnaps Julia. ISBN 0-941483-10-X   8.95

SAPPHISTRY: THE BOOK OF LESBIAN SEXUALITY by
Pat Califia. 3d edition, revised. 208 pp. ISBN 0-941483-24-X   10.95

CHERISHED LOVE by Evelyn Kennedy. 192 pp. Erotic Lesbian
love story. ISBN 0-941483-08-8   9.95

THE SECRET IN THE BIRD by Camarin Grae. 312 pp. Striking,
psychological suspense novel. ISBN 0-941483-05-3   8.95

TO THE LIGHTNING by Catherine Ennis. 208 pp. Romantic
Lesbian 'Robinson Crusoe' adventure. ISBN 0-941483-06-1   8.95

DREAMS AND SWORDS by Katherine V. Forrest. 192 pp.
Romantic, erotic, imaginative stories. ISBN 0-941483-03-7   8.95

MEMORY BOARD by Jane Rule. 336 pp. Memorable novel
about an aging Lesbian couple. ISBN 0-941483-02-9   10.95

THE ALWAYS ANONYMOUS BEAST by Lauren Wright Douglas.
224 pp. A Caitlin Reece mystery. First in a series.
ISBN 0-941483-04-5   8.95

PARENTS MATTER by Ann Muller. 240 pp. Parents' relationships with Lesbian daughters and gay sons. ISBN 0-930044-91-6   9.95

THE BLACK AND WHITE OF IT by Ann Allen Shockley.
144 pp. Short stories. ISBN 0-930044-96-7   7.95

SAY JESUS AND COME TO ME by Ann Allen Shockley. 288
pp. Contemporary romance. ISBN 0-930044-98-3   8.95

MURDER AT THE NIGHTWOOD BAR by Katherine V. Forrest. 240 pp. A Kate Delafield mystery. Second in a series.
ISBN 0-930044-92-4   10.95

WINGED DANCER by Camarin Grae. 228 pp. Erotic Lesbian adventure story.
ISBN 0-930044-88-6   8.95

PAZ by Camarin Grae. 336 pp. Romantic Lesbian adventurer with the power to change the world.
ISBN 0-930044-89-4   8.95

SOUL SNATCHER by Camarin Grae. 224 pp. A puzzle, an adventure, a mystery — Lesbian romance.
ISBN 0-930044-90-8   8.95

THE LOVE OF GOOD WOMEN by Isabel Miller. 224 pp. Long-awaited new novel by the author of the beloved *Patience and Sarah*.
ISBN 0-930044-81-9   8.95

THE HOUSE AT PELHAM FALLS by Brenda Weathers. 240 pp. Suspenseful Lesbian ghost story.
ISBN 0-930044-79-7   7.95

HOME IN YOUR HANDS by Lee Lynch. 240 pp. More stories from the author of *Old Dyke Tales*.
ISBN 0-930044-80-0   7.95

PEMBROKE PARK by Michelle Martin. 256 pp. Derring-do and daring romance in Regency England.
ISBN 0-930044-77-0   7.95

THE LONG TRAIL by Penny Hayes. 248 pp. Vivid adventures of two women in love in the old west.
ISBN 0-930044-76-2   8.95

AN EMERGENCE OF GREEN by Katherine V. Forrest. 288 pp. Powerful novel of sexual discovery.
ISBN 0-930044-69-X   9.95

THE LESBIAN PERIODICALS INDEX edited by Claire Potter. 432 pp. Author & subject index.
ISBN 0-930044-74-6   12.95

DESERT OF THE HEART by Jane Rule. 224 pp. A classic; basis for the movie *Desert Hearts*.
ISBN 0-930044-73-8   10.95

TORCHLIGHT TO VALHALLA by Gale Wilhelm. 128 pp. Classic novel by a great Lesbian writer.
ISBN 0-930044-68-1   7.95

LESBIAN NUNS: BREAKING SILENCE edited by Rosemary Curb and Nancy Manahan. 432 pp. Unprecedented autobiographies of religious life.
ISBN 0-930044-62-2   9.95

THE SWASHBUCKLER by Lee Lynch. 288 pp. Colorful novel set in Greenwich Village in the sixties.
ISBN 0-930044-66-5   8.95

SEX VARIANT WOMEN IN LITERATURE by Jeannette Howard Foster. 448 pp. Literary history.
ISBN 0-930044-65-7   8.95

A HOT-EYED MODERATE by Jane Rule. 252 pp. Hard-hitting essays on gay life; writing; art.
ISBN 0-930044-57-6   7.95

AMATEUR CITY by Katherine V. Forrest. 224 pp. A Kate Delafield mystery. First in a series.
ISBN 0-930044-55-X   10.95

THE SOPHIE HOROWITZ STORY by Sarah Schulman. 176 pp. Engaging novel of madcap intrigue.
ISBN 0-930044-54-1   7.95